SLICE OF TEMPTATION

A REVERSE AGE GAP ROMANCE

SUGAR AND SCOTCH DUET
BOOK 1

D.L. DARBY

For all the women who have carried the past with them. It's okay to hold on—but it's so beautiful when you let go.

CONTENT WARNING

This book contains materials that may be hard for some readers. Teenage pregnancy, off-page death from childbirth, cheating (not MFC or MMC), perceived cheating, and estranged parent.

Please do not hesitate to reach out to me on any platform to further inquire about these triggers.

Please read responsibly.

CONTENTS

THE TRUTH IS, EVERYONE IS GOING TO HURT YOU. YOU JUST GOT TO FIND THE ONES WORTH SUFFERING FOR.

-BOB MARLEY

PROLOGUE

GOD, GUYS ARE FUCKING DUMB. WELL, LET ME rephrase that, high school guys are dumb.

I would have given him forever.

Devon Eddison.

We'd been together since we were kids. Grew up next door to each other. I'll never forget when he asked me to be his girlfriend while we chased frogs through my backyard when we were just ten.

"There's no one else I'd rather catch frogs with, Rylee. All the other girls are stupid. Well, except for Rysta, I guess. But only 'cuz she's your sister."

I thought it was so romantic. Our parents thought it was so cute. My younger sister was devastated because she'd been infatuated with Devon ever since he shared a cookie with her when she was four.

No one thought it would last. One year turned into two. Two into four. And by seventeen, I was ready to spend the rest of my life with him.

But Devon had monsters in his closet that I think a lot of boys do at that age. Back then, they were taught to hide their feelings and keep them inside. Even though I feel like I gave him the safest space he could ever have to truly be himself, he decided he couldn't talk about his fears of the future with me. Maybe because I was supposed to be a part of it.

Or maybe because Cherie Johnston was just easier to talk to that day on the beach.

Senior skip day–a day when the seniors ditch school and find something to do for fun collectively. We'd all decided to head to Whittle Beach, down the road from Daytona Beach. I was so excited to spend the day soaking up the sun and watching Devon's rippling abs while he played catch with the other members of the football team.

Much to my dismay, I caught the twenty-four-hour flu and wasn't able to go. It wasn't a huge deal. Whittle was less than twenty minutes away from our small town Sandridge, so I could go whenever I wanted. But a few of the guys on the football team had fathers in high places and were able to get a bonfire permit, so it did suck that I would miss out on that.

Said guys also had filled water bottles with various alcohols. So, as day turned to night and everyone got drunk, Devon found himself in a tangled web of bad decisions with the dark-haired girl known as Cherie.

She was sweet, quiet, and artistic. And everyone

knew she had a bad situation at home. Her dad was abusive, and her mom needed to leave him but didn't have the courage. Cherie and I had actually gotten along really well until the bonfire happened. Until she and Devon fell into a deep conversation over a water bottle full of Southern Comfort and woke up tangled in each other's arms amidst the white sand and dune grass. They weren't even discreet about it, which meant that the whole senior class knew before I did.

No less than fifteen people had told me before Devon had called me himself. I was in such denial that he would do something so shitty–and shocked that I was hearing about it from everyone else–that I hadn't even entertained the idea of calling him. And my twenty-four-hour flu turned into forty-eight hours with all the stress I'd been under.

It was overwhelmingly embarrassing going back to school that following Monday. Everyone whispered behind my back, sending me looks of pity as I slowly passed through the halls with my face hidden behind my mocha-colored hair. Some people even said I deserved it because Devon was so devastatingly hot, and rumor had it I hadn't given him my virginity yet.

That tidbit of gossip was a lie, but I didn't owe anyone that information.

Devon had kept trying to talk to me every chance he could, but I refused to speak to him. It affected the relationship our parents had with each other, they'd been friends for so long but it was awkward and none of them knew what to say to each other.

Then the real kicker happened. Cherie ended up being pregnant. She at least had the grace to tell me before it got around to the rest of the school. But it was all very dramatic. It happened in the hall during classes, with my best friend by my side and Devon a few feet away.

My best friend at the time, Lucy, had been digging her nails into my arm so hard I swear it was the only thing that held me up during the traumatic moment. And when Devon had tried to comfort me, she had jerked me away and held up a finger in a warning to stop as she yelled at him.

It was very à la Charlotte from the first Sex and the City movie–when Big tells Carrie that he's sorry he couldn't get out of the limo to marry her. I felt a lot like I imagined Carrie did at that moment. I didn't say anything as I allowed Lucy to lead me away from them to the office, where I called my mom to pick me up.

Seventeen was so young, and I didn't know what I had done in my short life to deserve the amazing parents that I had. But all it took was a brief conversation with them, and it had been decided that we would leave Sandridge and move a few hours North. I couldn't bear to show my face back at school. I couldn't stay and watch as Cherie's stomach grew big with Devon's child. The child that was supposed to be mine when I turned twenty-five, according to the plans we'd made.

Later, I would hear that Devon started drinking heavily and got kicked off the football team. I'd hear that his parents sent him away to military school after a string of run-ins with the cops.

Later, I would hear that Cherie died during childbirth, and it was what would finally prompt her mother to leave her abusive father, taking the newborn out of town with her when she went.

Later, I would amend my earlier statement back to the original one.

God, guys are fucking dumb.

CHAPTER ONE
TWENTY-FIVE YEARS LATER

Rylee

"HEY, WHAT ARE THE FLAVORS FOR THE Caketails this week?" the sultry voice of my best friend, Sadie, drifted through the doors that led from the kitchen to the bar.

Seconds later, she appeared holding a clipboard, working on what I assumed was the menu that we switched up every week. Her sleek blonde A-line bob had shifted to cover the majority of her face as she held the clipboard up and squinted at it.

I laughed. "You need to get your eyes checked, Sade. If you can't read that piece of paper, I'd say it's time for reading glasses, babe."

"Get fucked. Caketail flavors, please," she responded without looking up at me.

"Oh, I intend to," I replied as I sealed the lid on a tub of RumChata-infused buttercream. "Tonight, as a matter of fact. Tinder date. Nine at Pascal's. So you'll need to close up the bar. Flavors for the week are Horchata and Mexican Hot Chocolate."

I turned to survey the sparkling stainless steel that made up most of the kitchen, making sure it was spotless for the guys that come in the evening to do the small plate appetizers we offer when the bar is in full swing.

"Please tell me it's not with birdman." Sadie finally looked up from the clipboard, her bright green eyes aglow with mirth.

I rolled mine in return. "Yes, it's with Bill. Don't call him birdman. Dammit, now that's all I'm going to be able to think of," I moaned as I threw my head back in a mock sob.

"It's all you would have thought about anyway. Because it's all he talks about," Sadie said. She tossed the clipboard on the counter before she leaned against it and crossed her arms under her chest.

"Look, he's nice, okay? I feel like I can take him back to my place, give him a ride, and send him home to his birds." I grabbed the tub of lemons and stacked them on another one full of limes so we could continue our conversation while we cut fruit out on the bar. Sadie followed me as I turned to push my way through the double doors that led back out to the front.

"He doesn't give stalker vibes. He gives sad, lonely, I won't give you the best fuck of your life, but I'm good for right now, and I'll leave you alone after vibes."

"Well, now that doesn't sound very promising," a rich tenor dripping with amusement rang out behind me. I turned so fast that the lemons flew out of the tub I carried and all over the lower counters, knocking into glasses and rolling onto the floor.

Scotch-colored eyes stared at me from the other side of the bar out of a tanned face covered in what looked like a week's worth of stubble. The whitest teeth I'd ever seen on a man flashed behind full lips that were turned up in a heart-stopping grin.

The man reached over the marbled cream-colored bar top to extend his hand in greeting as his other one turned the trucker hat on his head backward, his thick chocolate hair that looked silky to the touch popping out above the closure. "I'm Chance. Tom hired us to redo the landscaping around the building. Just wanted to stop in and introduce myself. Maybe grab a few sandwiches for lunch, see what all the fuss was about."

I stared at him blankly as the seconds ticked by, and he gave me a weird look as he dropped his hand. Why couldn't I do anything? It was like I'd been frozen in place and couldn't move, couldn't talk, could barely breathe.

He looked slightly familiar, but I knew I'd never seen him before because he was obviously younger.

Sadie laughed behind me, and the noise shocked me out of my stupor. "Sorry! I'm Rylee. This is Sadie," I nearly shouted as I practically threw the fruit tubs on the counter and wiped my hands on my apron before extending my hand.

"What fuss did you hear about us?" Sadie asked as Chance shook my hand. His skin was calloused, the sign of a hard worker, and warm as it gently engulfed mine. His eyes never left me, but I could feel Sadie's predatory feline grin behind her question without looking at her face.

"Just that you guys had some of the best sandwiches in town...and some of the prettiest owners. It looks like the latter part was definitely true," Chance answered with another grin. He hadn't dropped my hand yet and still hadn't shifted his focus to Sadie.

"Well, that sure is sweet of you. Melanie down there can get you situated with the sandwiches," she said, her voice dripping with amusement. "You're gonna have to drop Rylee's hand, though, so she and I can get the fruit cut before she has to leave to get pretty for her date."

"I think she's plenty pretty just how she is now." Chance dropped my hand gently and finally looked over to Sadie for a second before turning his gaze down toward where Melanie, our coffee and sandwich girl, was standing at the counter prepping cold cuts.

My heart did something weird in my chest. What was wrong with me? I didn't do this. I didn't get this tripped up over a guy. Not anymore. Not since....

"That's kind of you, really. If you need anything else-" I started but was cut off by a guy coming in and shouting to get Chance's attention.

"Chance! Let's go, man." The newcomer was a little taller but leaner than Chance, with midnight hair and eyes to match. He was wearing blue jeans with holes in them and a white shirt covered by a thin hoodie with the hood pulled up.

The man turned to walk back out while he pulled his phone out of his pocket, but then he glanced at Sadie and froze. Suddenly, a warm smile crossed his face as he shoved his phone back in his pocket and strolled over to stand beside Chance.

"Hello, lovely lady. I'm Tyler, your future husband," he crooned while leaning as far over the bar toward Sadie as he could get.

Chance laughed and shook his head. "Tyler is my business partner. Tyler, this is Sadie and Rylee," he said as he gestured to each of us. He took a few steps back, and I shamelessly ran my eyes down his body to take in the jeans that were a little lighter than Tyler's and a plain white tee that stretched over his muscles.

I turned to look at Sadie, who watched Tyler like a cat watches a new kitten it didn't want in the house. She held up the finger that sported her wedding ring set and replied saucily, "Married already, but thanks, pup."

"Ooh, spicy. I like women with a little kick to

them." He grinned as he hopped onto a barstool and leaned his elbows on the bar's smooth surface.

Chance tapped him on the back. "Come on, man. Quit playing. Let's get to work." He flashed me another smile as he slightly inclined his head and started to back away toward the door. "It was nice to meet you, Rylee."

"Yes, run along and get to work, Tyler," Sadie said.

At the same time, I responded, "Nice to meet you too, Chance."

"You can call me Ty," Tyler said, not moving from his spot on the stool.

"I'll call you pup. How about that?" Sadie crossed her arms and leaned on the bar as well, smirking at Tyler while she gave him a great view down her shirt at her ample breasts. They were naturally big and still bouncy for her age–a fact she was most proud of and spent as much time as she could showing them off with her clothing choices.

"Oh, come on, don't be like that. I like older women. You're like fine wine; you just get better with age." He smirked at her.

Chance hung his head, fully aware that commenting on Sadie being older wouldn't win Tyler any brownie points. They both looked like they were in their mid-twenties. Sadie and I, while looking good for our ages, if I did say so myself, definitely looked older than they were.

Sadie huffed and straightened up. "Are you even old enough to drink wine?"

"Tyler, let's go. Don't piss off the owners, man. Rylee, Sadie, I apologize for my friend's behavior. We'll be going now." Chance grabbed Tyler by the back of his hoodie and yanked him off the stool.

"Bye, wifey!" Tyler sang to Sadie as he walked backward since Chance still had a grip on him.

After he pushed Tyler out the door, Chance turned and looked back at me as he flipped his hat forward again. "Don't have too much fun with Mr. Sad and Lonely tonight."

He didn't allow me to respond before he disappeared, and Sadie gave a short laugh as she leaned her back against the bar and looked at me in astonishment. "What was that?"

"What was what?" I asked innocently as I grabbed a cutting board and a knife to start cutting up lemons.

"Babe, I haven't seen you act like *that* in a long-ass time. He was flirting with you! You could be going out with him tonight instead of birdman."

Ugh. Birdman. "He's way too young for me. He could have any hot piece of ass his age. Besides, I don't want to mix business and pleasure if Tom hired them."

Sadie grabbed another board and knife and started on the limes. "That is the saddest excuse I think I've ever heard in my life."

"Eh, it is what it is. I'm going to finish this and then get going if you don't mind. It's been slow today."

"Caw Caaaawww." Was her response before we both burst out in laughter.

CHAPTER TWO

"Damn, Tom was right, dude. They are hot," Tyler exclaimed while grabbing some hedge cutters from the back of our work truck.

Tom, the owner of the building that the bakery was in, had been making a piss-poor attempt at making the outside look as nice as the inside did. The shrubs were overgrown, the flowers looked half-dead, and there were hanging pots all around the building, which also housed dead flowers.

At night, the bakery turned into a bar. Who had hanging flowerpots outside of a bar? I almost wondered why he bothered at all and why Rylee and Sadie hadn't stepped in. But Tom was also a lecherous old man, so that might be enough explanation right there.

"What did he say their last names were again?" Tyler asked, pulling his hoodie off and throwing it in the backseat.

"I don't know, it's on the invoice in the front. Don't get too attached. She's married," I lectured. I'd actually never seen a woman turn Tyler's head that quickly. It figured it would be someone taller, older, taken, and wielded the ability to throw his shit right back at him.

"Tailor. Sadie Tailor. Why does that name sound familiar?" Tyler murmured, pulling out his phone.

"Stalk your girl later. Let's get to work. You start on that side, and I'll start over here. Let's just worry about cleaning up the bushes today."

"I'd like to clean her bush," Tyler snickered.

I rolled my eyes and laughed. He could be so damn immature sometimes, but I knew underneath that happy-go-lucky facade was an earnest man who had worn his heart on his sleeve too many times and was one heartbreak away from being ruined.

The sun hung high in the sky, and I could already feel the sweat dripping down my back. My thoughts drifted to Rylee as I got started on my work. Those cherry red lips and mocha-colored hair kissed with caramel. Golden-tanned skin and hazel eyes that looked like they held too much...*something* in their depths. She was breathtaking.

I hadn't had a serious relationship for a couple of years. There had been random hookups here and there, but nothing substantial. Women my age were flighty and shallow, and once they got to know me, they didn't stick around.

My mom–grandma who raised me, but I'd always called her mom–had consistently told me I had an old soul. I liked to sing karaoke and go out to early dinners so that my nights could be spent curled up in front of the TV with my cat and a book. I liked experiences over gifts. And I worked my ass off so that I could enjoy early retirement and travel when I was older.

Girls my age didn't care about any of that. They wanted to go out to clubs and out on yachts. They wanted expensive bags, spa days, and dressy dinners at fancy restaurants and didn't expect to pay for any of it. They expected you to worship the ground they walked on.

It was a major turn-off.

I wondered if Rylee was like that. If she was dating anyone that she expected to dote on her. But from the sounds of her conversation with Sadie, that wasn't the case. Rylee had to be older than me, though I couldn't tell by how much. I guessed she was maybe in her early thirties, at least less than ten years older. Maybe an older woman was what I needed.

I thought about her date tonight. Mr. Sad and Lonely seemed, well, sad and pathetic. She hadn't seemed too enthused by it, either. It sounded more like she was looking for someone to get her off and leave her alone after.

The first bush I'd started working on was looking

better, but the amount of dead shrubbery that littered the ground now was going to take more work to clean up. I was glad I'd marked off the whole afternoon for this project. Tyler and I ran and worked the business alone, but I was starting to think we needed to bring on a few more guys.

A gust of warm wind blew through the parking lot, knocking one of the hanging pots into my head. I tossed the hedge cutters on top of the now flat surface of the shrub and turned to start taking the pots down from their hooks. Looking over to where Tyler was, I noticed he was on his phone still, frowning down at the small screen. He'd at least managed to get two shrubs done.

A candy apple red Chevy Malibu pulled around from the back with Rylee in the driver's seat, putting on a pair of sunglasses. I'd been thinking of walking back inside to try and convince her to go on a date with me tonight. But it looked like I was too late.

She looked over, and her pouty lips turned up in a smile as she gave a small wave to Tyler, who had finally put his phone away and waved back. She pulled out of the parking lot–turning left in the direction of the beach, I noted–without so much as a glance in my direction.

"You think my new wife will bring us out sandwiches? I'm starving!" Tyler yelled over to me.

"Grab a protein bar from the truck. We're coming back for dinner tonight," I responded as I detached the last flowerpot.

Sadie had looked like she was all for her friend having a good time tonight. She'd watched our earlier interaction like a cat about to get a Squeeze Up treat. I'd bet anything she'd be willing to tell me where Rylee would be.

When Mr. Sad and Lonely couldn't deliver, I'd be there to sweep her off her feet.

A FEW HOURS later found us walking back into Sugar and Scotch with more on our minds than meeting the owners or sandwiches. It had picked up, the evening crowd busying the bar side while the lights were dimmed over the sweets and coffee bar on the other. It looked completely different at night. The dim glow from the chandeliers deepened the teal of the painted wood and cast a yolky glow on the cream marble of the counter.

There were no empty spots at the bar, but when Sadie looked up and saw us standing there, she gave me a knowing smile and cocked her head to where the bar curved at the end. Beyond that, there were multiple high tables made up of the same wood and the same stools as the bar. A few words from Sadie made two of the guys move to one of the tables without so much as a fuss, leaving room for Tyler and me to take a seat.

"Well, well, well. Look what the cat dragged back in. You boys did a great job on the bushes out there. Tom tries, bless his heart. He does his best to stay busy after his wife died, but I think even he knew it was a lost cause. No green thumb, that one. What can I get you guys?" she said as she wiped down the surface in front of us.

Now I felt like an ass for what I had thought about Tom earlier. Maybe it was just the sentiment of a sweet old man when he'd told me about Rylee and Sadie being pretty. I opened my mouth to order a drink when Tyler interrupted me.

"I'll take whatever Miss Sadie Tailor wants to make me," he said without as much enthusiasm as he'd had when talking to her earlier.

She narrowed her eyes at him and cocked her head. "How'd you figure out my last name?"

He waved it off and grabbed a drink menu lying off to his side. "It's on the invoice we got from Tom. What's a former model doing in a place like this?" his playful tone returned.

"Can I get a Jameson? Neat," I asked, ignoring Tyler.

"You want the location of Rylee's date to go with that?" Sadie asked with her feline grin as she made my drink. I smiled and nodded, but she placed a rocks glass in front of me and turned her attention back to Tyler. "I prefer the sun down here to the polluted air in New York."

"Bet you prefer the men, too, huh? Your husband's a dick." Tyler's comment made me choke on my drink, and I shot him a look that clearly said, *what the hell?*

Sadie bit out a short laugh and crossed her arms, her green eyes sharpening as she asked, "And what would you know about my husband?"

Tyler shrugged. "It's not a secret. Anyone with the internet could see that if they knew what to look for. Can I get a beer, please?"

Sadie looked affronted but turned and poured him a Budweiser on draft. She slammed it down in front of him, the glass mostly foam.

He smiled and took a sip. "Aww, baby. You know I love it when you give me head."

She was about to respond when I interrupted her. "Can you two resume whatever *this* is after you tell me where Rylee is?"

That feline grin was near feral as it turned to me. "Oh, you fell hard, didn't you, pup?"

"That's *my* nickname," Tyler pouted. Both Sadie and I ignored him.

"Look, I heard you guys talking about her date tonight. I was amused, so I listened for longer than I probably should have before making my presence known. She's hot and looking for a good time. *I'm* a good time."

"How old are you guys, anyway? God, I should have checked your IDs." She hung her head and pushed off the bar.

"How old do we look?" Tyler teased as he waggled his eyebrows at her.

"I'm twenty-five. Tyler and I own our business. I didn't go to college, but I think we're doing just fine without the extra schooling and the student loans. I haven't dated anyone seriously in two years, and I have a hunch that you're about to tell me I'm too young for her, but I think I'm just the right age. It was obvious we had a connection this afternoon. I just want the chance to explore that with her," I over-explained. I had a feeling I was going to need Sadie's blessing to get anywhere near Rylee.

Sadie gave a slow shrug. "I think anyone is better than birdman Bill. They're meeting at nine at Pascal's."

Well.... That was easier than I thought it would be.

"Birdman?" I asked.

"You don't want to know. They've gone out a few times now. Nothing's happened, but Rylee seems to think he's a safe choice to give that pussycat some action."

It was Tyler's turn to choke on his drink.

I mirrored her grin. "What's good to eat here?"

She raised an eyebrow at me. "It's almost eight-fifty, pup. I'd get going if I were you."

I shook my head and sipped my whiskey. "I'll eat first, then head over. Something tells me they'll still be there."

"And I'll stay here and help you close up shop, then we can go home together," Tyler said nonchalantly.

Sadie laughed and shook her head as she turned to grab us some menus. We ordered, and as she walked away, I handed Tyler a napkin to wipe the drool from his mouth.

Something also told me that these two would be causing each other a lot of trouble.

CHAPTER THREE

It turned out the third time wasn't always a charm.

I tried. Really, I did. I would be polite and continue the rest of the date but I definitely would not be going home with birdman Bill. I was on my third Black Cherry Cruzan and Coke while he was still sipping on his first Seven and Seven, talking about birds. He was always talking about birds.

I don't know what I had been thinking. He was so nice, but I wasn't desperate.

My thoughts drifted to scotch-colored eyes and a certain disarming smile. It had been a long time since a man occupied my thoughts as quickly as Chance had. We'd made a connection this afternoon. I knew I hadn't made it up. Even Sadie had sensed it.

"You know what I mean?" Bill's nasally voice interrupted my thoughts.

I blinked a few times and smiled. "Yes. I know

exactly what you mean," I lied. I had no idea what he'd been talking about.

He seemed to know that, too, because he flushed a shade of raspberry and suddenly found his drink very interesting. "I'm sorry I must be boring you with all my bird talk."

Not at all. "Yeah."

He looked at me in surprise, and I winced. Shit, I had meant to switch that thought process.

Bill recovered, blinkingly rapidly and stuttering as he asked, "W-well, how is...how is the bar d-d-doing?" He smoothed the side of his sandy blond hair down and scrunched his nose, making his thick mustache wiggle. He took off his wire-framed glasses and cleaned them while he waited for my answer.

I felt bad. I didn't want to be unkind, so I quickly nodded and took a sip of my drink before I answered, "It's going really well! The bakery is busy during the day, and the bar is doing even better and-"

I abruptly stopped when I noticed the man who'd just come through the door. Pascal's was busy on a slow night, so tonight it was packed with people playing darts and pool and getting ready to fill the area around the stage for Saturday night karaoke. But like some invisible tether that drew us to each other, his eyes immediately found mine amidst the over-crowded bar. Scotch to turtle shell green.

"Can you excuse me for a second?" I didn't give Bill time to answer as I stood and started making my way to where Chance was grinning at me. He looked good enough to eat in a tight black shirt and light wash jeans.

"What are you doing here? Did Sadie tell you where I was?" Had he really come looking for me? Butterflies fluttered in my stomach at the thought that maybe he'd also felt like we'd had a connection.

"Hi to you too, cupcake. I heard this place has karaoke tonight. I love me some karaoke." He grinned, and I knew from the look on his face that Sadie had, in fact, told him where I would be tonight.

"Karaoke? Really?"

"Birdman? Really?" he echoed.

Fucking Sadie. I was going to kill her.

I crossed my arms. "His name is Bill."

"I thought it was Mr. Sad and Lonely?"

"Are you really here for karaoke? Where is Tyler?"

He gave me a pointed look. "Where do you think he is?"

Probably annoying Sadie at the bar. "Okay, well, I'm sorry. I assumed you came here for...." I trailed off because it sounded stupid saying it out loud.

He grinned as he leaned down and whispered, "Maybe I did. Maybe I just came to sing."

AN HOUR PASSED, and I'd been keenly aware of every second of it. Chance had snagged a random seat near the stage and sipped whiskey while every young woman his age tried to shoot their shot with him.

Every single time he shook his head and pointed his thumb over his shoulder in my direction. And when the women would look around, confused, he'd just smile and shake his head again. I was too far away to hear whatever he would say to them, but he enunciated enough for me to read his lips.

Not interested. Taken. Waiting for someone.

And just when I was ready to make myself the bad guy and end Bill's incessant droning about American Oystercatchers, Chance sauntered up to our table. "Wanna sing with me?"

I looked back and forth between him and Bill. "Um...."

"Excuse me, but we're on a date. What are you doing? It's kind of obvious here," Bill stated, motioning between us.

"Oh, dude, I'm so sorry. I thought you guys were, like, cousins or something," Chance replied, looking like he wasn't sorry at all. He knew exactly what he was doing.

I snorted into my drink and tried to hide a laugh while Bill looked over at me incredulously.

"Seriously, my apologies. I'll let you guys finish up here, and I'll be over there when you're ready to start enjoying your night, miss." Chance pointed behind him to the karaoke stage.

I had to hand it to him. He had guts.

He didn't give me time to respond as he walked away and headed to the stage.

"Can you believe that guy?" Bill asked. But I barely heard him over the beginning chords of ABBA's "Take A Chance On Me."

No, he didn't.

Chance grabbed the microphone and started singing the first verse as he stared directly at me.

Yes, he did.

I laughed as his voice drifted out over the crowd and people started to sing along. He kept his eyes on me while he danced and sang, and I was vaguely aware that Bill was trying to get my attention.

Chance sang the line about the pretty birds flying away, and we shared a knowing smile.

"I'm sorry, Bill. This isn't going to work," I said as I gathered my things.

"Oh, dear. He's upset you, hasn't he? The scoundrel. Where is security?"

I left as he looked around for a security guard and made my way to the stage. Chance grinned down at me like the cat that got the canary, and I shook my head and gestured for him to get down.

As the fourth verse started, he passed the microphone to a group of girls who'd been singing along in front of the stage and jumped down.

"Ready to get out of here?"

I nodded as he grabbed my hand and led me out of Pascal's and over to a shiny black GMC Sierra.

"Get in, cupcake. I'm gonna take you to my favorite spot in town."

I glanced over at my Malibu and paused long enough for Chance to realize I was hesitant. "We could take your car if you'd prefer? Or do you want to follow me?"

It occurred to me that I had no idea who this man was. But, as he waited patiently for me to make a decision, I figured that Sadie knew who I was with, and if she hadn't heard from me in a few hours, she'd likely hunt us down herself.

"Your truck is fine. You can just bring me back later," I decided.

"Of course. I'll bring you back in the morning before work." He winked at me, flashing those straight pearly whites again.

And I shivered with excitement at his statement.

CHANCE'S favorite spot in town was a small beach area that you could access through or between the backyards of a ritzy neighborhood. The yards were immaculate, with large palms and clusters of bright-colored flowers everywhere. The street he pulled onto was quiet, and the house he parked in front of had its lights out.

"Are you sure we're allowed to be here?" I asked hesitantly before he got out of the truck and came to my side to open my door.

"Of course. These are clients of ours. They won't care if we go through the backyard. I do it all the time. They're barely home anyway," he answered. He grabbed a small blanket from the backseat and motioned for me to follow him to the side of the house, where he opened a small gate and ushered me through a rock path lined with lavender.

The backyard was just as beautiful as the front. Even more species of flowers grew all along the low fence, with white and pink dwarf pentas cuddled up in beds of small rock. A lime tree stood in the corner with a small wrought iron bench beneath it. Another gate led out to the white sand beach on the other side of the bench.

"It's beautiful," I said softly as Chance opened the gate and held out his hand for me to take.

"I thought you might like it," he said as I placed my hand in his. My cheeks warmed as his fingers wrapped around mine. Even though there was a light breeze in the air tonight, my insides turned to liquid heat as he pulled me behind him.

The waves collided quietly with the shore as we walked further out. The sun had disappeared, the sky now an inky shade of indigo with the stars scattered like glitter. Chance stopped before the sand got too pliable, laid out the blanket, and then sat down and patted the spot beside him.

I slipped off the pink pumps that matched my lipstick and left them at the corner of the blanket before slowly lowering myself next to him. I wore distressed light wash shorts and a silky navy blue halter that Sadie had bought me in New York. But a thought came and went within seconds: I wished I was wearing a dress because it was easier access than my current outfit.

Okay, ho.

"We should just get the elephant in the room out of the way," Chance started, pulling his knees up and loosely draping his arms over them. "I'm twenty-five. I know, it's young. But my mom tells me I have an old soul."

Twenty-five. Jesus. What was I thinking?

"I can tell that wasn't what you were expecting," he murmured. His eyes were intense glowing orbs of amber as he stared into mine, trying to read my face for my reaction.

I was still opening and closing my mouth like a fish out of water, attempting to speak but only able to make short guttural noises as I scrambled for something to say.

"I'm forty-two. God, I'm almost old enough to be your mother," I finally managed, shaking my head as I looked out at the water.

"Does it matter? Because it doesn't matter to me. I mean, really. I know you felt it, too, this afternoon. It was like we had this instant connection."

"Chance, you are—extremely good-looking. And charming. Of course, anyone is going to have an instant connection with you." My tone bordered on whiny, and I knew I *sounded* like I'd been let down after learning something was too good to be true.

"So give me a chance—get it? Give me a *chance*— to show you that I'm more than just another pretty face." He turned to me and grabbed my hand, rubbing his thumb over it.

I had to laugh at his theatrics, which caused him to laugh too. Twenty-five or not, we did have chemistry. "I mean, I can't believe I'm saying this, but I don't mind hanging out if you really want to spend your time with an old lady. I don't understand why you would, though."

He stopped laughing and said, dead serious, "Have you seen yourself, Rylee? You're stunning. You put the girls my age to shame."

I snorted. "Okay, Chance. What did Big Al put in your drink at the bar? You've known me for what? All of five minutes? That's *'let's go hook up in the backseat of your truck'* time. Not *'let me take you to my favorite spot in town'* time. Or is this just where you bring all the pretty girls?" I smirked and nudged his shoulder with mine.

He frowned at me and, for a moment, looked genuinely hurt that I'd even suggested it. "I thought we had a hell of a meet-cute earlier." He nudged me back. "That's how people start dating, isn't it? They randomly meet each other and decide they wanna spend time together. And before you know it, they're picking out wedding venues and which cake flavor tastes better.

"I'll totally let you handle the cake, since that's your area of expertise. But that means you have to let me handle the flowers. I'm thinking beach wedding. Peach and blue. But soft, muted peaches and blues, not bright ones. Roses, because no one wants roses at their wedding these days. And I'll wear beige if you really want me to, but I think I'd look better in navy. Like your top." He flicked the bottom of my shirt.

I laughed and looked at him in astonishment. "Wow. You really had that all planned out, didn't you?"

"Oh yeah, I've been thinking about it all day. You'll wear a dress made for the beach. You'll go barefoot with those cute little footless sandals. You'll sweep your hair up out of your face with a single clip, and later, when I peel the dress from your body, I'll take that clip out slowly and watch as your hair falls over your face while you're above me."

My insides tightened, and I squeezed my thighs together as his voice dipped lower, huskier. "Did you pick out how many kids we're going to have too?" I joked.

He let out a laugh and shook his head. "No kids for me. Wait, do you want kids?"

I shook my head. "I have an IUD to make sure that doesn't happen."

"See? Perfect. We can spend our years traveling."

"You seem pretty sure of this whole scenario," I said quietly. I realized my hair was falling over my face just the way he'd described. And as we'd been talking, he'd slowly lowered himself back, so he was stretched out on his side and propped up on one forearm.

He reached up with his other hand, cupping my cheek behind my curtain of hair as he brushed his thumb lightly over my bottom lip. "I *feel* pretty sure about it. I can't explain it, but I feel like we were meant to meet today, Rylee. Maybe it won't go past tonight, and maybe you'll wake up in my bed tomorrow and think you made a huge mistake. Or—perhaps we'll be standing on this very beach in a year, saying our wedding vows."

"I don't do relationships," I said against his thumb, which was still touching my lips. I hadn't been in a serious relationship since high school, as dumb as it sounded. I'd allowed myself to get hurt and had promised it would never happen again. No man had attempted to try once I told them I wasn't interested in one.

"And why is that?" Chance cocked his head to the side as he sat up a little straighter, his hand leaving my face to intertwine with the other resting on the blanket.

"Because you can't get hurt that way." I blinked a few times, snapping out of whatever trance I'd been in while I drowned in those pools of scotch, and looked back out to the ocean.

Chance didn't reply, but I felt him stand up, and I figured that was the end of our short-lived date. If you could even call it that. I was not, however, expecting to feel the slight shift of his pants hitting the ground.

I slowly looked up at his well-muscled legs, past his black boxer briefs to that deep v sitting right below abs that should be illegal. He'd peeled his shirt off as well and was smiling down at me, completely aware that I was shamelessly taking in his near-naked body.

"What are you doing?" I asked in shock. My body grew warm all over at the sight of him, and a tiny sliver of hope that I would still get lucky tonight shot through me.

"Skinny dipping," he said nonchalantly as he reached to remove his briefs.

At the sight of my stunned expression he stopped, laughed, and shook his head. "I'm kidding. I'm going for a swim." He started making his way down to the water, the muscles in his back rippling with every step, and called out over his shoulder, "You coming?"

CHAPTER FOUR

Okay, I was coming on way too strong with all the wedding talk. The panic in her eyes the moment I brought it up was as evident as the tension in her body when I started talking about being serious.

There was something more to this woman than just her surface beauty. I could tell someone must have really hurt her for her to be so guarded. And I certainly hadn't walked into her place of business this afternoon expecting to meet someone I wanted to take on a date so badly.

But everything about her called to me. She was gorgeous, sure. But she had her shit together. She owned a business—a successful one at that. And her age didn't matter to me. Because when she looked at me, it made me feel like I could be anything I wanted to be. Do anything I ever dreamed of doing.

I never believed in love at first sight. Not even

after growing up with loving parents—maternal grandparents—that claimed it was like that for them. Not even when my grandma insisted that my biological dad had experienced it as well before he went and fucked everything up like he always does.

But this? This feeling that Rylee gave me. It might just make me a believer.

So, if I wanted to explore that feeling, I knew from here on out, I would have to cool it with talks of weddings and the future.

I turned around when I got to the water's edge. The shallow waves lapped at my feet as I waded in slowly walking backward. Rylee had gotten up and stood in the sand just off the blanket, clearly trying to decide if she would join me.

I smirked at her, the water almost to my waist, when I stopped. "Don't tell me you're afraid of little ol' me? Come on now. Get your ass out here."

She rolled her eyes and shook her head as her bright pink-painted lips curled up in a smile. Slowly, she reached for the button on her shorts. So fucking slowly, she slid them down her toned thighs, never taking her eyes off me.

I swallowed thickly as she stood and stepped out of them. A hot pink thong covered her, just barely, lace and sheer enough for me to know she was smooth beneath it. She reached up to grab the tie behind her neck, still holding eye contact as she pulled it, and the top started to slide down her body, revealing a strapless bra in the same color and material as her thong.

Her breasts were full, rosy nipples peeked from behind the lace, and I couldn't wait to get my mouth on them. I was thankful my dick was underwater because it was rock hard at the sight of her, and I had to adjust myself as she started walking to the water with deliberate steps, hips swaying with each one. A playful look in her eyes now replaced the panic she'd had only minutes ago.

That's right, baby. Come play with me.

"I've known you less than twenty-four hours, and you've somehow managed to get me out of my clothes. I think that's a record," she said, voice full of devilish delight.

"Technically, you got yourself out of those clothes. I'll get you out of these ones, though." I smiled as I waded water. The waves were still small, and the ocean was shallow at this beach. I could stand up and only be chest deep. It was one of the things I liked about this area. It was secluded and quiet, and I could swim peacefully without fighting the bigger swells found at most other town beaches.

"You sure are cocky," she sang as she came closer. She was maybe five foot five inches to my six feet. All I had to do was reach out to pull her to me and press her body against mine, but she drew back with a grin when I attempted.

"I prefer confident. Hopeful."

She finally moved close enough and allowed me

to pull her into my body. My hand settled in the curve of her waist and tightened just slightly, enough to draw a sharp intake of air from her. I hitched one of her legs onto my hip, her body molding into mine in a way I knew would make her feel my erection now pressed against her belly.

"You're too young for me, Chance. We shouldn't do this," she said softly. Her hands found their way to my shoulders, contradicting her words as she brought the other leg up to press herself into me.

"I told you, age doesn't matter to me. But if it really matters that much to you, then we can let tonight be just about sex. You can decide in the morning if you want to see me again."

The undercurrent swayed and rocked us together, her body moving infinitesimally against mine. "Just sex?" she asked.

"If that's all you want." I rubbed my thumbs against her thighs where I held her and leaned down, lips hovering just over hers. "And if you want more, I will give you... *everything*," I breathed into her mouth.

Her eyes were still open when she tilted her head to brush her lips softly against mine. A feeling of complete contentment went through me like this was just *right*. Like we were exactly where we were meant to be at this very moment. As if she felt it too, she closed her eyes and kissed me harder, her hands moving to my neck and upward to grip my hair.

Her tongue was cherry flavored as it teased mine,

and her teeth nipped my bottom lip playfully before exploring my mouth again, and I groaned. The feeling of her against me in the water wasn't enough. I wanted more.

I pulled back, relishing the sound of objection she made. "Let me take you home?"

She nodded, no unsureness left in her countenance. "Okay. Take me home."

ONCE WE WERE BACK in the truck and headed to my house, I kept looking over at Rylee as if, at any moment, she would change her mind and tell me to bring her back to her car. But she looked relaxed, a content smile on her face as she leaned back in her seat, angled in my direction. Her legs were crossed as she bounced one heeled foot to the music on the radio. She had her elbow resting on the back of the seat, her hand bunched in her hair that was still half wet from the ocean.

She grinned when she caught me looking at her again. "Afraid I'm going to change my mind?"

I laughed nervously. "Something like that. Just admiring how good you look in my truck. Thinking about how good you're going to look in my bed."

She laughed lightly and shook her head. "You don't have to try so hard, Chance. I already agreed to go home with you."

"I ain't trying hard. I'm just telling you the truth. You're not used to getting compliments, are you?"

She shrugged. "They don't mean much when they're hollow and only used to get me into bed."

"Hey, you were the one who said just sex. If things go my way, I'll be showering you with compliments for as long as you let me."

I pulled into my neighborhood—a cluster of single-family homes that were all white concrete with beige brick accents and gray-tiled roofs. Tyler and I took care of the landscaping for some of the houses in the area, and I'd wanted to buy here since we started working on them. So, as soon as our business had taken off, I'd snatched one up as soon as it had become available.

"I should have asked this earlier, but are you allergic to cats?" I asked Rylee as I pulled onto my street.

"No, I love cats!" she exclaimed, uncrossing her legs and sitting up straighter as she surveyed the homes.

"Alright, good. That might have been a deal-breaker," I joked. "Cause I have a fluff ball who thinks he owns the place."

I pulled into my driveway and hopped out of the truck to open Rylee's door for her. I ran my hand up one smooth leg while helping her out, my dick growing half-hard at the thought that she would soon be out of her clothes and wrapped up in my sheets.

She kept her hand in mine as I led her inside.

Domino, my cat, greeted us with a cacophony of meows as soon as I closed the front door.

"Hey, buddy. Meet your new mom. Rylee, this is Domino." I reached down and scratched his head before Rylee swept him up in her arms.

"Oh my goodness! Aren't you just the prettiest kitty ever," she cooed in his face before cradling him like a baby.

He reached up and tapped his paw against her face before looking at me as if to say, '*I approve.*' She kicked her heels off, walking further into the house with him still in her arms as she looked around.

"This is nice. Are you renting? Or did you buy?" she asked.

"I bought it a year ago. Tyler lives a few streets down from here. We liked the area. No crime, friendly neighbors, good schools." I shrugged.

She coughed suddenly and set Domino down. "Good place to raise a family," she said softly.

I came up behind her and grabbed her by the hips, pulling her into me while I nuzzled her neck. "Good area to live in general. I said no kids, remember?"

She turned and captured my lips with fervor, her hands going to the hem of my shirt to lift it over my head like she didn't want to waste any more time talking. And that was perfectly fine with me.

My hands roamed up her sides to the tie at her neck, and I pulled it more roughly than I intended, earning a sharp gasp from her as I slipped the top down her body before fisting my hands in her hair.

I devoured her. Mapping every inch of her mouth with my own before roaming my lips down the side of her neck. She groaned and reached for the buckle on my belt just as I nipped at the hollow of her neck. She made quick work of shoving my pants down before she moved to take off her shorts.

I grabbed her by the waist and pulled her back into me once she stepped out of them. We started walking, lips never parting as I pulled her along the hallway and into my room. I felt the back of my legs hit the bed and finally pulled my mouth from hers. We both breathed heavily, eyes locked as I slowly reached around to undo the clasp to her bra.

As it fell away, my eyes lowered to her breasts while I reached up to grasp them in my hands and squeezed gently. I leaned down and took one in my mouth as her back arched up, and she placed a hand behind my neck and pulled me closer.

"Chance," she whimpered as I bit her nipple and then sucked it into my mouth. My other hand roamed down her body, and I cupped her pink lace-covered pussy, pressing my middle finger along her center to feel how wet she was.

She was fucking soaked.

Rylee threw her head back as I rocked my finger against her again, and I moved up to nip at her neck. "Does that feel good, baby?"

"Uh-huh." Was all she managed as I moved my

finger up to press against her clit. She sucked in a breath and made a mewling noise that almost had me coming right then. My cock was rock hard, and I was ready to be inside her.

But we had the entire night ahead of us.

I removed my finger, hands going to either side of her thong as I pulled it quickly down her body. I spun her around and threw her on the bed, pulling her back to the edge by her hips before I shoved her legs open wide and dropped to my knees to cover her pussy with my mouth.

"Oh, fuck," she said in surprise, arching her back. Her legs clamped around my head as she reached down to try to push me away. "Chance, I want you inside me."

"Not yet," I said against her as I grabbed her by the calves and pressed her legs up and wide. I sucked her clit into my mouth, flicking it with my tongue as I ran one hand down the inside of her thigh and pushed two fingers into her. She was salty from the ocean, and underneath that was just *her*.

She tasted fucking delicious.

"Oh my god," she said between labored breaths. Her hips pushed up, and I turned my fingers inside her to gently coax her back down. My cock strained so hard it almost hurt. "I'm going to come," she warned as I worked her clit gently between my teeth.

I pulled my fingers out and ran the flat of my tongue along her as she tried to close her legs around my head again. I reached down and maneuvered myself out of my boxer briefs, my cock springing free and swollen with need.

"I'm coming," she sang as I pulled my mouth off her and stood to sheathe myself inside her. She cried out, her back arched, and her legs wrapped around my waist as I thrust into her.

"It's like you were fucking made for me," I growled while she fisted the sheets. Her pussy was slick, but gripped my dick like it was welcoming it home. With each thrust, I pulled out nearly all the way before driving in again, the momentum moving us up the bed.

She pulled me down and kissed me, all tongue and teeth, hot and wet. Her heels dug into my backside before she pushed me up in a silent command. In a matter of seconds, she was straddling my cock and rocking into me while I still sat upright.

Rylee bounced on my cock, using my shoulders for leverage as she threw her head back as I hit that sweet spot deep inside her. "Does that feel good?" she asked between a series of whimpers.

"You have no fucking idea how good you feel, Rylee."

I leaned forward and placed open-mouthed kisses against her breasts while she rode me. She was fucking crazy if she thought I was going to let her go after this. No. This wasn't just going to be about sex. She was mine.

"What?" She slowed and looked down at me.

I realized I must have said that last part out loud.

I wrapped an arm around her tighter as she rocked against me gently, and I thrust up hard. "I said you're fucking mine."

I picked up speed and bounced her on my cock while her breasts bobbed up and down in my face. The angle allowed me to fit so deep inside her, and I knew after this, I'd never want to leave. My dick was perfectly content to make a home inside her sweet cunt.

She watched me, her eyes half-lidded as she leaned down to kiss me again. Sweat trickled down the side of my face as I pumped up into her, kissing her lazily until I felt my balls start to tighten.

"Fuck, Rylee, I'm about to come." I moved to lay her back on the bed so I could pull out, but she flexed her thighs around my waist and rocked into me harder.

"I want you to fill me up. Make me yours," she whispered against my lips.

It was the hottest thing any woman had ever said to me, and I swore loudly and came the hardest I'd ever come in my life. She moaned and threw her head back, rocking against me while my cock twitched inside her, filling her with my cum.

I kept pushing up into her, watching her face as she cried out and came for the second time. It was the most beautiful thing I'd ever seen. The little whimpers that escaped her mouth while she rode her high. The lazy smile that curved those luscious pink lips upward as she looked down at me again. She was a fucking vision.

We moved together slowly, and she laid her forehead against mine. Neither of us made any attempt to part. Her fingers ran lazy patterns along my shoulders while I stroked mine across her lower back.

"Well, I guess you *are* more than just a pretty face." She smiled and pulled her head back a little, running a hand through my hair as we slowed to a stop.

I laughed and squeezed her tighter to me. "That was just round one."

CHAPTER FIVE

Buttery shafts of sunlight streamed in and roused me from sleep. I didn't remember the last time I'd woken up after a night of sex and *felt* it. That sweet ache that reminded you that you'd gotten off over and over again.

And fuck, it had been good.

Chance had ravished me throughout the night. Every single round had been that sweaty, dirty-talking, come-so-hard-you-see-stars kind of sex. When he'd called me *his* in a primal fit of passion, he hadn't been wrong.

I was ruined.

There was no way I'd ever find another man who could fuck as good as Chance did.

I shifted, tangled in the sheets, and stretched. The spot next to me was empty, but I could hear the spray of the shower coming from the bathroom connected to his room. I sat up and took in my surroundings, having not bothered the night before.

Chance's bed was king-sized and had more pillows than I'd ever known a man to own. The duvet had been kicked off the bed at some point. As I stood, clutching the flat sheet to my body, I saw it was the same shade as the sheets, a dusty blue that bordered on gray. The same color accented the room in small ways—a lamp, a painting, a chair with a decorative pillow on the cushion where, upon further inspection, it seemed Domino napped from the stray black hairs scattered across it.

There was a long beige-washed dresser with a large tv on it that faced the bed, and a door that I assumed led to a walk-in closet next to it. The wall opposite the bathroom was made of floor-to-ceiling windows, with one that slid open and led out behind the house. There was a small swimming pool and a table with a few chairs next to another glass door that looked like it led into the kitchen. The entire area was enclosed by a low brick wall with screens that attached to the house to keep out the bugs and other unwelcome intruders.

Domino was curled up on the brick ledge next to a screen door that led to the rest of the backyard. I opened the sliding glass door and stepped out. There were a few lime trees scattered between Chance's house and his neighbor's and a small swamp beyond their backyards with more homes on the other side of it.

I walked over to Domino, dragging the sheet behind me as I yawned. "Hey, pretty kitty. Good morning."

He stood as I came closer and stretched as I reached out to scratch his head. He was huge and had fluffy black hair that was soft as a baby duck. His big green eyes appraised me as I scratched down his back and then under his chin.

Something moved on the other side of the screen, and it took me a few seconds to realize what it was.

I screamed.

Domino startled and ran off as I backed away quickly and tried not to trip over the sheet. I turned to run back into Chance's room as he ran out of the bathroom, water dripping everywhere as he clutched a towel around his waist.

"What?! What happened? Are you okay?" he asked me in a rush of concern.

"There's a fucking gator out there that was trying to get Domino!" I yelled and pointed to where I'd just been.

Chance blinked, then straightened and started to laugh. I didn't find what was so funny. I'd grown up in Florida and lived here all my life. I knew alligators often roamed people's yards. But gators trying to eat your cat shouldn't be something you laugh at.

"That's just Gary. He's my water puppy," Chance said before he leaned in and gave me a short kiss. "Good morning, by the way."

"Water puppy? He was...he was trying to eat Domino," I said, confused.

"Nah, they're pals." Chance secured the towel around his waist and grabbed my hand, leading me back outside. Domino had returned and was pacing back and forth in front of the screen door while *Gary* lounged on the other side.

He was a juvenile, long and lanky, on the verge of filling out. He was probably four feet once I took a good look at him. That was four feet too much gator for me.

"Alright, Gary. Back to your swamp you go, bud. You're scaring my girl here," Chance said as he opened the screen door and stepped out.

"What are you doing?! Are you *insane*?!"

I watched as he walked around the alligator, grabbed it by the tail, and headed to the swamp. Gary just opened and closed his mouth a few times–slowly, not in a threatening way–and let Chance drag him off.

Domino scratched at the screen door and meowed like he wanted to go with, and I shook my head. "You guys are crazy."

I STEPPED into the warm spray of the shower and moaned. My body was sore from the previous night's activities, and Chance had told me I was welcome to shower while he made us breakfast. I don't think I'd ever had a guy make me breakfast the next morning.

Or maybe I'd just made an excuse to hightail it out of their homes or tell them to leave mine before breakfast could even be discussed.

The water felt amazing and soothed my muscles. And I was relieved to find that Chance had salon-quality shampoo and conditioner, not that three-in-one nonsense that a lot of guys use. I briefly wondered if it was left over from an ex or if his mom had just taught him the importance of good hair products.

Once I was done, I walked back out into the bedroom. Chance had laid out a pair of boxers and a plain white t-shirt for me to throw on in case I didn't want to wear my clothes from last night.

I smiled as I picked up the shirt and held it to my nose to smell it. Why was it that men's clothes always smelled like their cologne? Even after being washed.

Once I was dressed in his clothes, I walked down the hall to where I could hear Chance in the kitchen, singing along to a song playing over what sounded like a surround sound system. There was a small area halfway down that was open with everything a cat could possibly want to entertain it. Multiple cat trees were placed around the room with random cushions and toys strewn all over the floor. On the walls, it looked like Chance had created an interactive system for Domino to walk along and play. Opposite the hall on the other side of the open space was a floor-to-ceiling sliding glass door that led out to the pool.

Everything in the house was decorated in cream with soft blues and gold. There was a bathroom at the end of the hall, and when I came around the corner, the house opened up into a large living room with an open-concept kitchen and dining room area. There were two more doors on the other side of the house that I assumed were a laundry room and possibly another bedroom.

The dining room was surrounded by more floor-to-ceiling windows with a sliding door that led out to the patio where the table and chairs were that I saw earlier. The kitchen was all stainless steel with beautiful black-marbled quartz countertops.

All in all, I'd say Chance had good taste in home decor.

"Hungry?" his voice interrupted my thoughts.

"Starved. And surprised, if I'm being honest. You cook?" I climbed onto one of the stools in front of the breakfast bar attached to the island that housed a sink and dishwasher.

"I do. My mom taught me. Well, she's my grandma, but she raised me, so I call her mom," he explained as he flitted around the kitchen. He set a glass of what looked like fresh squeezed orange juice in front of me, followed by a bowl of yogurt with little dishes of granola and fresh fruits.

"You can start with this. The quiche should be done in about forty minutes."

"Quiche? Chance, this would have been fine," I said around a mouthful of yogurt.

"Hey now, I gotta keep trying to impress you so you'll stick around." He smiled at me as he cut up fresh parsley.

I grinned as I took a sip of my juice. "I think after last night, I can stick around for a little while."

He stopped what he was doing and looked at me as he raised his brows. "Really?" he asked as he popped a piece of kiwi in his mouth. I nodded as he walked around the island and pulled me into a searing kiss, almost causing me to fall off the stool.

The kiss grew heated quickly, our hands ready to rid each other of our clothes and go another round right in the kitchen. I pulled back and asked, "You said the quiche still had forty minutes?"

He shrugged. "More like thirty-five now." His eyes dipped back to my mouth before he captured my lips again, this time pulling my legs around his waist so he could walk us back to the bedroom.

"I think that's enough time."

CHAPTER SIX

"Oooh, someone got laid last night. I take it things went well?" Tyler questioned, grinning at me as I walked into our small office later that afternoon.

I'd gotten Rylee off twice before the quiche had finished cooking. Once by my mouth and again on my cock just before the timer had gone off. I would have called in if it weren't for her insisting she had to be at the bakery today because *Sundays were their busiest day of the week.*

I smiled and shook my head. "I'm gonna marry that woman someday."

Tyler pushed a pair of large framed glasses up his nose and rolled his eyes as he punched in numbers on a calculator and entered them into our computer. He had always been good at keeping our accounting up-to-date with how busy we were. "Ask how my night went," he said in a tone I knew all too well.

I had left him at the bar with Sadie when I went to find Rylee. Any other woman probably would have fallen at Tyler's feet and begged him to take them home, but even if Sadie weren't married I had a feeling she wouldn't be like any of those women. "How did the rest of your night go?"

"She kicked me out. Like literally right after you left. She let me finish my beer, barely talked to me, and then told me to get lost," Tyler explained in a voice that was happier than I would have expected for what he'd just said.

I laughed and sat at my desk. "You seem happy about that."

"It's all foreplay to me, buddy. I'll bet Sadie hasn't been properly dicked in a while. All that built-up sexual frustration? It'll explode at some point, and I'm gonna be right there when it does. Maybe we can have a double wedding." He shut the book and leaned back in his chair.

"You think I'm kidding about Rylee, but I'm not. I'm telling you, she is going to be my wife. She's fucking perfect. Everything I've ever wanted in a woman," I told him as I clicked on my computer to look at what we had coming up for the next week.

"Damn, Chance. You've known her for twenty-four hours, and you're already whipped. She must have been a real animal in bed."

"There is just something about her, Ty. I can't explain it. I've never wanted someone so bad. And the sex was fucking great. I still can't stop thinking about the things she said in that bedroom. The way she looked in my clothes-"

"She spent the night? Damn, you smooth talker, you. I honestly didn't think she'd cave that fast," Tyler interrupted.

"We just have good chemistry. And I'll admit, you and Sadie do, too. But, Ty, be careful, man. Okay? She's married. I don't want to see you get hurt."

Tyler shrugged and pulled up the hood on his gray zip-up. "Nothing can hurt me, Chance. You know that. You, on the other hand. You be careful too. These older women might want to play for a little bit, but it makes you wonder why Rylee isn't married or already in a relationship."

"She said she doesn't do relationships. That way, she can't get hurt. I think someone really fucked her up in the past, and she's afraid of that happening again. So I have to prove I'm not gonna be that guy."

"And what if you find that you don't like her all that much when you actually get to know her? What if she's got skeletons in her closet you aren't willing to take on?" Tyler asked.

"I can't imagine finding out anything about her that I wouldn't be okay with. Off-topic, we need to set up some interviews for this next week. We're getting too big to be doing this ourselves," I said.

We started our business, B and M Landscaping, when we were twenty-one. Neither of us wanted to go to college. My grandfather had done landscaping all his life and taught us everything we knew, and Tyler just had a knack for numbers and business. His father used to be a big businessman before he died tragically in a car crash when Tyler and his sister Ashlee were younger.

So, with help from my family and the money he'd saved from his parents' life insurance, we decided to go into business for ourselves. We enjoyed what we did. We both liked being outside and turning people's yards into art.

"Agreed. I've already called some of the applicants to set up interviews. You gonna be around for them, or should I expect you to disappear on me?"

I frowned at him and gave him a look that said, '*really.*' "Of course, I'll be around for them. Don't worry, Tyler, I'm not gonna disappear from the face of the Earth just because I met someone. We have a business to run, just like she and Sadie do. They'd probably get annoyed if we were around all the time anyway," I joked.

But as I checked my watch and realized the lunch rush should be just finishing up, I also realized that Rylee hadn't given me her number when I dropped her off this morning. Which meant that I was going to have to go back to the bakery if I wanted to talk to her again.

"Up for a sandwich?"

SUGAR AND SCOTCH looked like they were fifteen people deep at the sandwich bar, but Melanie looked calm and composed as she artfully made people's lunch. There was another group in front of a giant case filled with sweets, a girl I didn't recognize was behind it placing items in boxes and taking money.

Sadie was behind the bar where a few people were sitting to eat. She looked up when Tyler and I walked in, a smile on her face when she saw me–a frown when she saw him. To his credit, Tyler didn't say a damn thing as we took a seat.

"Back already? Geesh, from the sound of it, you guys had quite the night. I was honestly surprised to see Rylee come into work this morning," Sadie joked. Her eyes flit to Tyler for a second, but he was leaning back in his stool–hood up, hands in his pockets–watching Melanie work on the other side of the room.

"Yeah, I forgot to get her number this morning when I took her back to her car. I'm surprised to see you here. Didn't you close up last night?" I asked as I looked around for Rylee. I still didn't see her, so I assumed she was back in the kitchen.

"I'm always here. I barely sleep—Rylee's in the back. Let me grab her. But, I'm warning you, she's not going to like being interrupted on a Sunday. She's busy baking and decorating today. I don't think she's ever taken a weekend off in the three years I've known her," Sadie remarked as she pushed her way through the doors I now knew led to the back.

Rylee had told me she needed to come in to work today, but she'd never mentioned anything about not wanting to be disturbed. Surely she had realized that we'd forgotten to exchange numbers. But it still made me pause to wonder if perhaps I shouldn't have come by.

Then she came through the doors, and I knew I would never have been able to stay away.

Her hair was piled on her head, pieces falling around her face. Her lips were bright pink again, and her skin looked flushed. There was a smear of something across her cheekbone that was iridescent and shiny. She wore a pink frilly apron over a yellow short-sleeved top and white jean shorts. And as she came around the bar, I had to laugh at her bright teal heels.

"How do you manage to work in those things?" I laughed as I reached for her.

She gave me a tight smile and awkwardly returned my hug like we hadn't spent the morning with my head between her thighs. "Years of practice. What are you doing here?"

"Well, it occurred to me that we forgot to get each other's numbers this morning. How am I supposed to ask you on another date if I can't get ahold of you?" My hands were still on her waist, but she looked uncomfortable, so I let her go and took a step back.

"Is everything okay?"

She looked around quickly as if she were making sure we weren't causing a scene. "I just wasn't expecting to see you here. We just said goodbye a few hours ago."

Rylee would barely look me in the eye as she spoke, and I suddenly felt very self-conscious. "I'm sorry, I didn't mean to overstep. I thought we were on the same page, but apparently, I was wrong."

I stepped back and heard Tyler curse under his breath as he pushed his stool back. I had no idea what had changed in the few hours we'd been apart, but I felt like I had been punched in the gut. I caught the look on Sadie's face like she didn't know what was causing Rylee's behavior either. But I just shook my head and turned to leave. I could find a time to talk to her later. I shouldn't have bothered her at her job.

"Stop. Wait. I'm sorry, Chance. You didn't do anything. We are on the same page. I'm just.... I'm not used to this. I honestly didn't think–I thought once you got what you wanted that this would be over." She looked as nervous as I felt and kept looking around to ensure no one was paying atten-tion to us.

Was she serious? Had I not proven to her that I wanted anything she'd be willing to give me? She was the one who said she didn't want a relationship.

It hit me then.

She didn't want a relationship. She had said just

sex. And here I was, standing in front of her less than four hours after we saw each other last because I didn't have her phone number. She must have thought I was needy and pathetic.

"No, Rylee. I thought I made myself pretty clear about where I stood. But you're right. I shouldn't have come today. I know you made it clear what you did and *didn't* want."

"Do you really want to keep seeing me?" Her voice sounded small, unsure.

I walked closer to her and reached up to lift her chin so that she looked me in the eyes when I said, "I told you I would give you everything if you let me. I meant it. So, no. I'm not going to leave you alone now that I got what I wanted. There's still a hell of a lot more that I want from you. And I intend to take it all."

I crushed my lips to hers, and she responded fervently. We kissed until someone whistled and another person catcalled. She broke the kiss at the sound, and we both smiled as she tried to hide her face against my chest.

"I'm sorry. I'm just really confused. I know what I said last night and what I said this morning. But, if I'm being honest. You scare me, Chance. Because for the first time in my life, I almost called in today just so I could stay with you. That's a huge deal for me."

"I told her she should have. Work? Or sex all day? Doesn't seem like a hard decision to me," Sadie quipped.

"Bet you're ready for one of those days, aren't you? Just say the word, and I'm your man," Tyler shot at her in his normal jovial tone.

"Shut it, pup."

"Look, Rylee. I told you where I stand. You told me where you stand. So, I will follow your lead on this, okay? Because if you let me take the lead, I will want to be near you all the time. If space is something you need, just tell me. Just communicate. If I smother you, if you feel like I'm trying to push a relationship, just tell me if I'm too much," I told her quietly.

I straightened up and let go of her. There weren't as many people in the place now, so I motioned for Tyler to get in line at the sandwich bar. "Now, Ty and I are gonna grab lunch and get out of your hair."

"Don't you need my number?" Rylee asked.

"Give it to me when you're ready," I responded. I didn't say anything else as Tyler and I got our food and left. Rylee had gone to the back again, and Sadie had followed her.

So, when I got back to my house, I didn't know how she managed to get her number on a card that I found slipped into my bag.

CHAPTER SEVEN

Rylee

"WANNA TALK ABOUT IT?" SADIE ASKED IN A
soothing voice as soon as we were back in the
kitchen.

I sighed and set my arms on the edge of the
counter where I'd been making a mess with edible
dust before Chance had shown up. "I don't know
what's wrong with me. That was so stupid. I acted
like an idiot."

"Which makes me wonder if this is what you
needed the whole time I've known you, Ry. A
younger man to take that edge off." Sadie nudged her
shoulder into mine, her tone light.

"Why am I like this? Why do I let things affect
me so astronomically? Yet another reason I don't
want a relationship. It's like I can't feel things
normally. Either I don't care, or I care too much," I
rattled on until Sadie put a hand on my arm.

"It's okay to feel things, Ry. Even if you feel them to the extreme. I know we've only been friends for a few short years, but you were happy when you came in this morning. Like, really happy. I don't know what changed between the time you came back here to decorate and the time Chance showed up-"

"I was left alone with my thoughts," I interrupted her. I grabbed the discarded piping bag that was half full of cotton candy-colored frosting and pulled a tray of vanilla cupcakes closer.

"Okay, so I have to babysit you until you come to terms with the fact that you hooked up with a younger man who wants to worship the ground you walk on." Sadie lifted herself onto the counter and grabbed a stack of cake boxes that needed to be put together for orders that would be picked up later.

"He's pretty intense. So is Tyler," I said as I looked at her from the corner of my eye.

Sadie smiled, it was small and not meant for me to see it, and then it was gone in a second. She shrugged. "They're young. We're hot, we have our shit together, and we're successful. I'm married, which poses as a challenge. And something tells me Tyler likes challenges."

I smirked at her as I finished piping the cupcakes. I reached for the opalescent luster dust and some fondant pearls and began to arrange them in random patterns. "You know I would never judge you if you wanted to have a little fun, Sade. It's not like Scott is quiet about his whereabouts when you're not in town."

"Just because Scott wants to be a horrible husband doesn't mean I have to be a bad wife. I'm content to spend his money and stay here, where I'm happy."

"And free to do what you want. Just saying." I wanted her to know that I would never judge her for indulging the way her husband did. Sadie needed to be fucked just as badly as I did. All that pent-up frustration makes a woman cranky. I would know.

My thoughts drifted to the night before and that morning. Remnants of phantom touches snaked along my skin. Chance had made me feel alive in a way no one else had in a long time. I'd lost count of how many times he had made me come. And he'd eaten my pussy like it was his last meal. Guys my age rarely did that anymore.

My thighs clenched at the memory, and I pulled my phone out. Then threw my head back and groaned as I remembered that I didn't have Chance's number either. I laughed at the irony.

"He'll call or text soon. Don't worry," Sadie said as she finished the stack of boxes and hopped off the counter to head back out to the bar.

"Sure. If I didn't scare him away by acting like a complete bitch," I said more to myself than her.

LATER THAT NIGHT, as I folded my legs underneath me and settled back into my couch with a glass of rosé, I rechecked my phone. I had set it down while preparing a chicken breast and salad for dinner and willed myself not to look at it until I finished my meal. This time, I was elated to see I had a message from an unsaved number. I quickly opened it and smiled when it was Chance.

> I'm lying in bed right now, and all I can think of is how I wish you were next to me.

> This is Chance, by the way. In case you might think it was another guy lying in bed thinking about you.

I rolled my eyes and saved his number before replying.

> Thanks for the clarification. You're in bed early.

> We have an early start. It's gonna be a busy week. We're interviewing people Thursday and Friday. We've never had people work for us before, but the operation is getting too big for just the two of us.

That's really great! You'll be able to expand more if you get some good guys under your wing. The work you guys did outside the bakery was beautiful, and the backyard of that house was gorgeous. You're really talented.

Thank you. You know what else I'm talented at?

My lower belly flooded with warmth, and it wasn't from the wine. I had a feeling I knew where this conversation was headed.

Karaoke? You are an exceptional singer ;)

LOL. Thank you, but that's not what I'm talking about.

Okay, I'll bite. What else are you talented at?

My phone buzzed a second later to show that Chance was calling me. My heart quickened, and I picked up my glass, hitting accept as I walked down the short hall to my bedroom. I had a feeling I was going to want to be in my bed for this.

"Hello?"

"Where are you?" Chance asked, his voice low and husky.

"About to get into bed," I answered. I put the

phone on speaker and set it down so I could get out of my clothes and into pajamas.

"Are you getting undressed?"

"Maybe."

"When you're naked, I want you to get into bed and lay back against your pillows. Put me on speaker," he commanded.

"You're already on it," I replied a little breathlessly. I quickly finished removing my clothes and climbed into bed, already wet between my thighs. "Okay, I'm in bed."

"Good girl. I want you to think of this morning. Think of how good it felt when my tongue slid along your pussy. How it felt when my cock stretched you, and I was buried deep inside you."

I moaned quietly as the sound of his voice alone sent shivers down my body. Gently, I ran my fingers down along my breasts, over my nipples, and rubbed my thighs together before letting them fall open.

"Did it feel good this morning, Rylee?"

"Yes," I moaned as my hand moved lower. My pussy was soaked as I ran two fingers over my clit and down through the wetness while the other hand tweaked my nipple. "Fuck, Chance. I wish you were actually touching me right now."

He chuckled lowly. "Trust me, baby. I would much rather have those luscious lips wrapped around my cock than my hand."

The thought of him touching himself turned me on even more. "Yeah? Are you imagining your cock sliding slowly between my lips while I'm on my knees?"

I swirled my fingers against my clit. Gently, then harder, then gently again. I thought about Chance licking and sucking me that morning. I thought about how the next time we saw each other, I wanted to drop to my knees and take every inch of his cock into my mouth and return the pleasure he'd given me multiple times already.

"Fuck, Rylee. I love it when you talk like that. I imagined what I would do to that pretty mouth all day. Do you think you can take all of me down your throat, baby? I don't think you can, but I'm going to enjoy watching you try." The noises from his end were undoubtedly him pumping himself, and I wondered if he used lotion or lube. The thought sent a fresh wave of pleasure through me, and I arched my back, pressing my hips into the bed in search of a pressure that wasn't there.

"I want you to slide your fingers into that pretty pussy. Two of them to start, then stretch yourself wider with a third. Use your thumb to rub your clit. I can hear how wet you are, Rylee. How turned on you are right now."

I did as he told me and pushed three of my fingers in to stretch myself wide while my thumb gathered and spread my arousal over my painfully throbbing clit. My body thrummed with a pleasure so intense it almost drove me to the point of tears while I worked myself to the sound of his voice.

"I can hear you too, Chance. Are you thinking about how it felt when my pussy gripped your cock? Are you thinking about how you filled me with cum over and over again? Are you imagining it's me coating your cock?"

I heard him suck in a breath and groan as he picked up his pace. The wet slapping sounds synched with my thrusting fingers, and I angled my hips up to get deeper. I moaned loudly, my head tilting to the side closer to the phone.

"Fuck, yes. I can't wait to fuck you again. All the different positions I want you in. All the dirty things I want to do to you. Get on all fours, baby. Ass in the air while you continue to fuck yourself."

Again, I did exactly as he told me. I was so close, and it sounded like he was too. "Tell me what you're going to do to me," I whimpered.

"There won't be an inch of your skin that isn't marked with my cum. My cock is going to stretch that beautiful mouth just like it will your cunt. Eventually, maybe even your ass, if you'll let me. Or maybe we'll just have to get a toy for back there, hmm? So I can fuck you in both holes at once. Tell me, baby, how does that sound? Would you like that?"

"Fuck, Chance, I'm going to come," I gasped as he talked. I fucked my fingers faster and used my other hand to rub furiously at my clit as I pressed my cheek harder into the bed. My moans grew louder, and I didn't hold back because I knew he liked it when I was loud. I imagined him bchind me, instead of on the other side of the phone, about to shoot his cum all over my back while he watched me fuck myself.

"Fuck yeah, baby. That's what's going to get you off tonight, isn't it? You want me to fuck your pussy and ass at the same time," his voice strained.

I came hard around my fingers as a liquid fire released through my veins, and I heard him swear as he came too. I couldn't think of a time when I had come so hard by myself. Where I had gotten sweaty and lost all my inhibitions without someone physically there with me.

Neither of us said a thing as we breathed heavily and came down from our highs. I was a sticky mess and would have to change the sheets before I went to bed since there was now a wet spot underneath me. I rolled over, not in the mood to post-coital cuddle my phone, and took it with me as I headed to the bathroom and turned on the shower.

"So, when will I see you again?" I asked casually, like we hadn't just had the most incredible phone sex of my life.

He laughed, and I could just picture him shaking his head while he got out of bed, cum all over his stomach, and it sounded like he was turning his shower on too. "Since Sundays are off-limits for you, how about Saturday? I've got the perfect thing in mind."

"Saturday sounds good to me."

"Great, I'll pick you up at ten. Wear something for being outdoors. Goodnight, Rylee."

"Goodnight, Chance."

We hung up, and I took my time showering for the second time that day before I slipped into a camisole and shorts and got into bed. I fell asleep thinking of him doing what he said he was going to. I'd never let anyone close to fucking that part of my body.

But fuck, I would definitely let Chance do it.

CHAPTER EIGHT

A<small>LL WEEK</small> C<small>HANCE AND</small> I <small>ENDED EVERY NIGHT</small> on the phone. We didn't always have phone sex. Sometimes we would just fall asleep listening to each other talk. It was nice to have someone to talk to, not that Sadie wasn't great company. But she knew everything about me.

It was nice getting to know someone and letting them get to know me. I'd forgotten what it felt like. To make a connection like the one I was making with Chance.

I kept thinking that the age thing would get in the way. That something would come up that showed how young he was, and then I'd be questioning my sanity all over again. But, to his credit, Chance was more mature than most men my age.

He hadn't stopped back by Sugar and Scotch for the rest of the week, and by the time Saturday rolled around, I was eager to see him. He had told me to wear something for being outdoors, so I had thrown on black bike shorts, sneakers, and a black form-fitting workout shirt. I nervously played with a lock of hair while waiting for him to pick me up.

Chance wouldn't tell me where we were going but said my clothes needed to be fitted. A million possibilities went through my mind while I waited, but when I finally saw his truck pull into my four-plex's parking lot, I still had no idea what he'd planned.

"Mmm, you look good enough to eat," he greeted me as he pulled me into his arms and crushed his lips to mine.

Instant warmth flooded my body, and my toes curled when his fingers gripped the bare skin between my top and shorts as he trapped me between him and his truck. His kisses were slow but deep, and he tasted like mint.

After a few moments, he pulled away and asked, "You ready?"

I pouted as he moved to open the door for me. "Are you really not going to tell me where we're going?"

"Would it make you feel better to know that Sadie knows where I'm taking you?" Chance asked before shutting my door and jogging around the truck.

I looked at him with a clearly annoyed look on my face. Sadie Tailor the traitor was what I was going to call her when I saw her at work tomorrow.

"You told Sadie?" I asked as he hopped in and pulled out of the lot.

"Okay, so I had to make sure you wouldn't absolutely hate me when you find out what we're doing today. If I'm being honest, Sadie doesn't think you'll be the happiest woman alive when you figure it out. But, I wanted to take you to do something you've never done before–something no other man has tried to take you to do, at least to Sadie's knowledge. And I think you'll love it if you just have an open mind." He grinned at me.

"Okay, Chance. I'm in the truck. We're on our way. Just tell me what it is already!" I nearly shouted with anticipation. My heart hammered inside my chest. If Sadie thought I wasn't going to like it, then why on Earth would Chance think I eventually would?

"Okay, okay, okay. I'll tell you. But only if you promise not to try and make a run for it while the truck is still moving," he said as we pulled up to a stoplight.

He must have read my mind as I stared at the red light glaring back at us because he kept looking over at me until the light turned green and the truck moved again before he said, "We're going skydiving."

I FIDGETED NERVOUSLY as I tried to pay attention to the educational video I was being made to watch. The owner of the skydiving company was a client of Chance's, so he had arranged it to where it would be just us going up in the plane instead of in a group. But that didn't make me any less anxious.

"Relax, baby. I've done this fifty times, at least. Tyler and I got certified at Freefall University at CSC while visiting his sister a few years ago. I promise you're in good hands," he whispered into my hair before pressing a kiss to my temple.

"I'm terrified of heights, Chance. I don't know why the hell Sadie would give you the green light for this," I bit back. I was angry with them both. But, I had to admit a small part of me wondered what it would be like–to jump out of a plane and marvel at the world below.

Sadie had ignored all the messages I'd sent her since I learned where we were going. She'd be getting an earful, for damn sure.

Chance pulled me tighter into him and nuzzled my ear. "If we get up there and you really don't think you can do it, then that's okay, we'll come down in the plane."

"How many other girls have you brought to do this?" I asked as I crossed my arms and leaned away from him as the uneasy thought rolled across my mind like a tidal wave.

He chuckled, removing his arm from around me as the video ended. "None, Rylee. Besides Ashlee, Tyler's sister. And the females I had to jump with to get licensed. But I haven't brought one woman to this place or even asked. You're the first."

I softened at his statement but couldn't help but still feel put out. My chest ached from how anxious I was, and tears pricked my eyes as an instructor helped me into my harness and gear a few minutes later. I knew that Chance would call it off if I really wanted him to, but I stayed silent as we loaded onto the small plane.

The instructor, Patrick, sat in the front with the pilot, Stephen, chatting to each other while Chance and I sat alone in the back as we ascended. Oddly enough, flying had never bothered me. Just things like being at the top of tall-ass buildings and staring out the windows or parasailing and hang gliding–not that I had done the latter two.

"How high up are we going?" I asked Chance quietly as I wrung my hands together in my lap and tried to focus on my breathing. The ache in my chest wasn't getting worse, but it certainly wasn't getting any better.

"The standard is ten-thousand feet. We'll be in the air for about forty-five seconds. I promise it will be one of the most beautiful things you've ever seen." He reached over and grabbed my hands, rubbing his thumbs across my wrists. "You doing okay?"

I breathed deep through my nose and exhaled through my mouth before I nodded. "I can do this."

He gave a sharp nod of his head. "That's my

girl." Then he moved up to the front, where Patrick was waiting to hook us together.

I pulled my hair back into a ponytail while Patrick told me all the things to expect, which was everything Chance had already explained to me. It made me feel a little better to hear someone validate him. Not that I didn't trust him. But, if I were being honest, it *did* make me feel better.

"Is it going to hurt when you pull the parachute?"

Both Chance and Patrick shook their heads as Patrick maneuvered me so he could strap Chance in at my shoulders and hips. "No, the harnesses are designed to be comfortable. And I'm gonna make it as smooth as possible for you, babe. No tricks. Just a standard jump," Chance replied.

"Chance here has done this plenty of times before. You're in good hands," Patrick said as he finished securing us together.

"Thanks, man," Chance said as he shook Patrick's hand.

"No problem. You know what to do. I'll signal when you're good to go," Patrick said before he made his way back into the cockpit with the pilot.

Chance gently guided me to the opening in the side of the plane. We didn't seem like we were going that fast, but the air was chilly, and my hair started to whip around my face from my ponytail. Panic settled in my chest as I looked out at the landscape below.

So far below.

I shook my head and tried to push back, but Chance had a hand braced on the frame of the plane, and he held his ground. "I can't do this," I shouted over my shoulder to him.

His arm tightened around my waist, and he leaned into me, lips ghosting over my ear. "Just relax, babe. Take a deep breath."

The arm around me shifted, his hand moving lower over my shorts until his fingers settled right over my clit. I sucked in a sharp breath as he started to circle them, rubbing that tight bundle of nerves through the fabric.

I had another moment of panic that had nothing to do with being so high up in the air and everything to do with Stephen and Patrick seeing what Chance was doing. But as if he could read my thoughts, he whispered, "They aren't paying attention, Rylee."

My body was tense as he wound me tighter and tighter. I reached up to grip his arm that was holding onto the frame of the plane door as my breathing became shallow and the familiar heat between my legs grew stronger.

God, this was so fucking hot. *He* was so fucking hot.

And doing a great job of taking my mind off the fact that we were about to jump out of a plane.

"Close your eyes," he ordered. I did as he said, throwing my head back on his shoulder as I felt that intimate pressure start to build, and everything else melted away.

"Good girl," he whispered, "now let go." His words made my orgasm rip through me, and I felt like I was falling.

And as I opened my eyes, I realized we *were* falling. Chance had jumped out of the plane as I had come. I opened my mouth to scream, but my voice died as I took in the scenery below.

It really was one of the most beautiful things I'd ever seen.

CHAPTER NINE

Rylee

RELATIONSHIPS MEANT COMMITMENT, AND commitment meant giving someone your heart to tear to shreds if they wanted. Since high school, I hadn't particularly cared to give my heart to anyone again. I knew it seemed stupid, holding onto something that happened so long ago—when I was a teenager, at that. But, in my adult life, no one had ever made me feel the way my high school boyfriend had, so I didn't even entertain the thought of making any of those situationships long-term.

So, it was a wonder I found myself here, seven weeks after Chance got me to jump out of a plane, baking in his kitchen like I lived here. I had my own toothbrush in his bathroom. Domino, Gary—yes, Gary—and I had developed our own morning routine. And Chance had just let it all happen naturally. He hadn't pushed, prodded, or asked. He'd just let me make the decisions on my own.

I was dating a twenty-five-year-old.

And I was perfectly content with it.

I pulled open the oven as the timer went off, a batch of blueberry lemon muffins filling the kitchen with a light, sweet aroma. I was trying some new recipes on my day off, and Chance had said I was welcome to bake at his place if I didn't want to do it at the bakery alone.

Sadie had gone to New York for the week. She'd been asked to be part of an article about former models and their views on how the industry had changed since their "glory days." She had arranged it so that her husband would be out of town on business while she was in the city.

We decided to close Sugar and Scotch for a few days, take a small break and have it deep cleaned—something we tried to do every few months. So, it worked out that Chance didn't mind that I occupied his home while he was at work.

Two cakes were already cooling on a baking rack: a Victorian sponge and vanilla champagne. I set the blueberry lemon muffins next to a small batch of cranberry orange. Most of the time, my muffin flavors were sweet, so I was venturing into the fruitier side of the small breads since I also made an array of cupcake flavors that were so similar.

I'd debated making cookies. Chance and Tyler had hinted that peanut butter oatmeal was their favorite, but cookies had always been my sister's thing, and I didn't particularly care for them.

Growing up, my sister Rysta and I always baked with our grandmother. It's where I got my passion for it. I had always known I wanted to be a baker when I grew up. So, as soon as I finished high school, I left for Paris and spent a year wandering the streets and eating at every boulangerie and pâtisserie I could find.

Domino meowed and snapped me out of my reverie of warm croissants and tiny decadent desserts. I looked down at him as he flicked his tail back and forth, watching me like he usually did when I baked. I shook my head as I put a pan of ginger pear, the last of the new muffin flavors, in the oven.

"No sweets for you, pretty kitty. But you can have a lick of a Squeeze Up." I opened the fridge to grab the one I'd opened the day before for him. Chance was very serious about him not having too many treats in a day. Apparently, it was too easy for cats to become overweight, and he loved this cat like it was his child.

It was an unusually gray and gloomy day for this time of year. The rain outside had been pouring on and off all day, causing the air to be muggier than usual. I'd asked Chance why he and Tyler worked when it rained, but he had said they spent their day meeting with clients and making purchases when the weather was like this.

They'd been busier lately. After hiring four more guys to help out, they expanded and picked up more clients, and it made me happy to see them succeed with their business.

After Domino finished his treat, he padded out to the back patio and started to groom himself. I poked my head out to make sure the screen door was shut, remembering the last time I hadn't shut it properly after grabbing a few limes off the tree right outside of it.

"Mmm. Something smells good," Chance said as he came around the corner and kissed my cheek.

"I made key lime pie," I replied as I cleaned up my mess from earlier.

Chance walked over to where the patio door was open, a habit I'd formed so Domino could come and go as he pleased while I baked.

"Fuck! Rylee, you didn't close the door all the way!" Chance called out, clearly panicked.

A rush of adrenaline made my heart stop for a moment as I instantly thought Domino had gotten out. I rushed out to the patio and promptly stopped to avoid running into Chance, who was just standing there.

"Domino didn't get out, did he?" I asked as I stepped up to his side.

But I could see that Domino had not gotten out.

Gary had gotten in.

Chance and I both cocked our heads as we stared at what was probably the oddest thing I'd ever seen.

Gary was floating in the swimming pool, as gators tended to do from time to time. But curled up on his back was Domino. Like it was the most natural thing in the world for these two creatures to lounge about in the pool together.

"Huh."

Chance echoed my sentiment as we stared, arms crossed, trying to figure out how on Earth we would extract Gary from the pool.

Once I knew the door was firmly shut, I returned to the kitchen to clean up. I'd gotten flour dust all over the counters, and it covered the digital picture frame that sat at the end, full of pictures of our various dates over the last few weeks. I had gotten it for Chance as a gift, seeing as he had no photos at all in his home save for one of him and Tyler on their first solo skydive jump that was attached to the fridge with a magnet.

A photo of us on a fishing boat was currently displayed on the frame. Chance's well-muscled body, shirtless and tanned, against the Miami turquoise-colored waters in the background as I held up a grouper—the first fish I'd ever caught—with a large smile on my face.

"My dad loves to fish. I've just never been inter-ested." I stretched out in my chair and pulled my wide-brimmed hat a little lower over my face.

"You gotta at least try, Ry. Come on. It's fun! We can grill it up tonight for dinner. It tastes better when you're the one who caught it. We didn't come down for the weekend for you to just lay out and tan. We

could have done that at home," Chance scolded playfully.

He was baiting a large, heavy-looking hook with squid, and I scrunched my nose at the smell. The day was beautiful, and there was a light breeze on the water. Unfortunately for me, that breeze carried the stench of the bucket of bait Chance had brought along on the boat.

"If I try and catch something, will you let me just enjoy the sun for the rest of the day?"

He laughed. "If that's what you really want, babe. But something tells me if you catch one, you're gonna be hooked. No pun intended."

We both had laughed as I finally gave in and let him teach me how to fish. And that damn grouper had fought me so hard that Chance had been the one to reel it in. And he'd been true to his word and let me soak up the sun the rest of the day.

But he was right, and the fish had tasted way better, knowing we were the ones who caught it.

The Backstreet Boys "Everybody" started to play over the speaker, and I leaned over to turn it up. There was nothing better than playing your favorite songs and singing as loudly as you could while you cleaned up.

The picture on the digital frame changed as I wiped the flour from it. Chance, Tyler, Sadie, and I smiled at the camera from Tyler's living room as he hosted a game night two weeks ago, and I snorted, thinking back to that night.

"Wow, pup. Nice digs. I won't lie. I expected a messy bachelor pad," Sadie voiced as she looked around his house.

The layout was exactly like Chance's, but where Chance's home was decorated in lighter tones, Tyler's home was darker. Deep hematite-colored accent walls and black leather furniture were scattered throughout the place. The flooring was a dark walnut, and glass tables accented the living room and kitchen.

Funnily enough, it reminded me a lot of how Sadie's penthouse in New York was decorated. Which I knew was all her and nothing Scott had a say in.

"Aww, wifey! Don't worry. I haven't been bringing any ladies here. Besides, they'd be deterred by the portrait above my bed even if I were stupid enough to bring them home," Tyler crooned as he smiled at Sadie.

I looked at Chance and raised a brow as I took a sip of my pinot noir. But he looked at Tyler with a huge smile and an incredulous look. "Ty, you didn't, dude."

Tyler just kept grinning at Sadie, who had an annoyed look on her face. "Which one is your room, Tyler?" she grit out.

He jumped up from his place on the couch and clapped his hands. "I thought you'd never ask! This way!" he exclaimed jovially as he led her down the hall to the main bedroom.

"Smooth." I shook my head while Chance threw an arm around me.

"Three.... Two.... One...." he counted down.

"What the actual fuck, Tyler," I heard Sadie say.

"I think I like it better when you call me pup," Tyler responded, and I could hear the amusement in his voice.

"What did he do?" I whispered to Chance, but he just shook his head.

"Go see for yourself."

I set my glass on a coaster and headed to Tyler's room, raising my hand to cover my mouth when I walked in and saw what the big deal was. "Oh, dear lord."

Above his bed was a giant photo of Sadie. One of her modeling photos from when she was younger. She was dressed in pearls, and nothing else. It was very à la Kim Kardashian, but now I know where Kim got her inspiration from.

And it was huge. Like something you would see in wealthy people's homes who hung giant portraits on their walls over the fireplace of themselves.

"Take. It. Down," Sadie growled as she reached over and smacked Tyler upside the head.

I promptly turned to leave to let them sort it out, and as I sat back down with Chance, I looked at him and smirked. "How long, do you think, until they sleep together?"

He shook his head and pulled me in for a quick kiss. "I give it another couple of months before he wears her down."

"Babe? I say this with the utmost respect, but I

don't think I'll be taking you to karaoke anytime soon," Chance's smokey tenor cut through my thoughts and, perhaps, *slightly* off-key singing.

I let out a small yelp as I jumped and whirled around, throwing the dishcloth I held at him. "You scared me!"

He was leaning against the island counter, watching as I had been dancing around, looking utterly delicious in a gray muscle tank and his backward hat. Butterflies erupted in my stomach as a heat ignited lower. "I called out your name, but you were busy attempting to summon a demon."

The butterflies and heat instantly vanished. "I am NOT that bad a singer!"

He laughed and came around to pull me into his arms. "Okay, you aren't that bad. But if your singing was the only thing keeping us alive...? Well, I'm sorry to say we'd die quickly."

I grabbed his hat, turned it around, and pulled it down over his eyes as he laughed. "That's it. I'm packing up all my treats and taking them to the bakery." I pushed his chest and tried to back away, but he bent me backward as he fixed his hat and kissed me hard.

"I'm just giving you shit. I love coming home to you in my kitchen screaming like a banshee." Another kiss. "I think you should just move in." And another. "I could get used to doing this every day." A caress of his tongue against mine. "You should think about it." A nip of my bottom lip. "But I'm not pushing."

He released me and grinned as I stared at him with a dreamy expression. Chance reached behind me and picked up the lemon-shaped timer I had bought for his house, then buried his face against my neck. "When this goes off, why don't we go for a swim in the pool?"

The way he said it, so low and gravelly against my skin, had that heat rushing back between my legs, and I had to bite my lip to stop a moan from escaping. He licked and nipped at the hollow of my neck, and I could feel his erection against my lower belly as he pressed me against the counter.

"I'm going to go rinse off in the shower. Tyler and I had to deliver a ton of trees and shrubs to a client for tomorrow. I'm sweaty and not in a good way." He winked at me and pulled away.

"Okay, as soon as these are done, I'll join you," I said as he started walking toward the bedroom.

I thought about what he'd said as the heat settled, licking at my insides slowly like a cat padding back and forth as it got ready to pounce. I glanced at the timer; five more minutes until the muffins would be done—five minutes to wonder if I was ready to share a home with him.

Sadie had asked me once if I wanted to move in with her. She owned a one-point-two million dollar condo on the beach, and I had still said no. I liked my space. I liked having a quiet spot to unwind at the end of a long day with no one to chatter at me or judge if I drank a bottle of rosé to myself. Not that Sadie, or even Chance, would judge.

It was just different, coming home to your own space versus coming home to someone else. I had been on my own for a long time. Even now, I only stayed at Chance's no more than three or four nights a week. And sometimes even that was too much.

Chance would likely set up the guest bedroom for me if I told him how I felt about it. A place where I could go to be by myself if I needed. Hell, Chance would probably go to the guest bedroom and let me have the rest of the house if I asked.

Domino wound his way around my feet as he looked up at me and meowed. "What do you think, pretty kitty? You think I should move in?"

Meow.

"You don't think it's too soon for that?"

He sat and flicked his tail back and forth, offering a shorter, quieter mewl before he dropped to the floor and stretched out on his back, his way of asking for a belly rub.

A knock on the door interrupted my conversation with the fluff ball I'd come to love as my own. Domino quickly stood and padded over to the door as if he were going to answer it himself. I swore he was more like a dog than a cat.

I could still hear the shower running as I crossed the hall to the front door. I figured Chance wouldn't care if I answered it. Especially not if this was to become my home too. The doorbell sounded as I raised my hand to turn the knob, and I frowned. Whoever was on the other side was impatient.

Domino stepped closer, tail swishing back and forth like he was gearing up to bolt, so I put my foot out to block him as I opened the door. "Can I help–" The words died in my throat as it seized up, and my heart started to beat erratically in my chest.

Stormy blue eyes, like the clouds after the rain, stared back at me in equal shock. Flashbacks from my childhood flooded my brain. Meeting as kids. Birthday parties. Admitting we both liked each other. Our first kiss. Our first time together.

Him breaking my heart.

Devon Eddison stood on the other side of the door, taller than I remembered him being. His hair was cropped short on the sides and longer on top, a far cry from the shag it had been the last time I'd seen him. He'd filled out, no longer the lean-muscled football star, but the swells of his arms barely fit the sleeves of his black t-shirt.

"Rylee?" he asked in stunned awe, as if he was unsure it was really me standing in front of him.

"Devon. What are you–what are you doing here?" My voice was stronger than I felt, and I was thankful it didn't waver with the anxiety spreading its way through my veins rapidly.

"I could ask you the same thing. I must have the wrong house. But how crazy is that? That I showed up on your doorstep? How have you been?" He shook his head, and a smile crept onto his face. Like no time had passed.

Like nothing had ever happened.

Annoyance, laced with anger, started to replace the anxiety. "This isn't my house. It's my boyfriend's."

My younger, hotter boyfriend. So, ha.

His smile faltered for a second when I didn't answer his question and made it clear I had no intention to. He looked down at his shoes for a moment before shaking his head and looking back up. "I get why you wouldn't want to talk to me, Rylee. I'm sorry. I honestly thought this was the house I was looking for. I'm just trying to get a hold of my son."

Ice pierced my heart in a short quick stab, and I had to fight to swallow the lump in my throat. All these years later and to have that reaction when he talked about the kid he had with the girl he cheated on me with.

It still fucking stung.

I heard a noise from down the hall, and a second later, Chance's voice rang out. "Babe, I heard the doorbell. Is someone here?"

I didn't miss the way Devon froze. And I smirked in petty triumph as I heard Chance making his way down the hall. I hoped he turned the corner with water still rolling off his abs, wearing nothing but a towel.

"Yeah, but he's got the wrong house," I responded. Devon's eyes searched behind me as I heard the shrill ding of the timer go off in the kitchen.

"Okay, I'll grab those," Chance said as he came around the corner. I turned to look at him, and to my dismay, he'd thrown on a pair of boardshorts, but he was still dripping wet, at least. He looked every bit the picture perfect man to throw in Devon's face.

Chance spared us a glance just as I turned to give Devon a victorious smirk.

"Dad?"

"Chance?"

Straight horror was written all over Devon's face and mine now, I suspected, as my grin dropped and my world slowed with those two words. I suddenly felt Chance's presence at my back as he reached above me to grab the door.

I twirled out from under him as Devon's eyes kept pinballing back and forth between us. "What the hell is this?" he asked.

"What are you doing here?" Chance asked, utterly unfazed by Devon's behavior.

Meanwhile, I had fled to the kitchen as I quickly did the calculations in my head. Chance was the right age. His mother had died during childbirth, and his grandmother had raised him. Facts that I should have noticed had it not been for the little details attached to them.

Like how he'd said his grandparents had raised him. But Cherie's mom had left her father. How was I supposed to know she'd remarried? Their last name wasn't Johnston, like Cherie's. It was Birchem. He was the right age but was I supposed to question every man in his mid-twenties? He was estranged from his dad, who had gotten his mom pregnant in high school. And when he was younger his dad was always getting into trouble, so he was never around. I had heard through the grapevine that Devon had been shipped off to military school because he had spiraled after Cherie decided to keep the baby.

Chance was Cherie and Devon's son.

I wanted to throw up.

"Hey, what the fuck do you think you're doing?" I heard Chance ask, and a few moments later, a large hand gripped my forearm to spin me around.

"Get your hands off her," Chance growled as he stepped in between us.

"What are you doing with my son, Rylee? Is this your way of getting back at me? Are you insane?" Devon roared as he glared at me over Chance's shoulder.

Hot waves of nausea rolled through me, and I started to breathe deeply through my nose and out my mouth as I replied, "I didn't know. I swear."

"You two know each other?" Chance asked as he turned slightly to look at me. As soon as he saw my face, he frowned. "What is going on? How do you two know each other?"

Devon ignored him as my stomach clenched in preparation for relieving itself. I gripped the counter behind me as sweat started to bead at my hairline.

"Do you want to tell him, or should I?" Devon asked between clenched teeth.

"Tell me what? Rylee, are you okay? Will you just tell me what's happening here?" Chance pleaded. He grabbed my chin and tipped my head up, worry etched on his handsome face.

I stared into his eyes as tears started to prick mine. The other shoe had finally dropped. I knew, deep down that he was too good to be true. "Chance, I...Your dad and I...."

Chance searched my eyes for a few moments as I struggled to tell him what I was struggling to come to terms with myself. Realization dawned slowly, like watching him put a puzzle together in his head. When the final piece clicked, he released me and took a step back, his hands suspended in the air as he pointed to both of us and looked back and forth between Devon and me.

"You guys have slept together?"

A few stray tears slipped down my cheeks as I glanced at Devon, who was still looking at me with his jaw clenched. I shook my head and turned to brace my arms on the counter. The warmth from the oven reminded me that the muffins still needed to be taken out, so I wiped the tears from my face and turned it off before removing them.

Their spicy, sweet scent caused nausea to roll through me again, and I knew I needed to get out of there.

"You could say that," Devon finally spoke up

behind me. "Rylee and I dated in high school. We were together when your mother and I–when we conceived you."

A few moments of silence hung in the air before I heard Chance whisper in disbelief, "It was you. My grandmother told me about you but she never said your name."

Then he laughed. It was loud and harsh and full of disbelief. I felt it in my chest like arrows had pierced my heart. "This is a joke, right? You do tend to show up from time to time and try and fuck up my life, don't you, Devon? Rylee, tell me this is one of those times." His voice was angry, strained, and I knew it wasn't directed at me, but I felt responsible for it anyway.

Without answering him, I darted out of the kitchen, grabbing my purse from the island and slipping on my yellow pumps before I flew out the door that was still wide open. I heard both Chance and Devon shout my name before they started to argue with each other as I fled down the driveway and got into my car.

This was why I didn't do relationships. I'd been subconsciously waiting for Chance to do something to ruin it–ruin us. I hadn't thought about the possibility that it would be me who did the ruining.

CHAPTER TEN

I watched Rylee peel out of my driveway, the tires squealing with urgency as she raced away. As soon as her car disappeared, I questioned whether or not it had been the right thing–to let her leave. I was just as shocked as she and Devon, but I knew the second she went through the front door that it didn't matter.

Rylee was still my future, even if she was my dad's past.

"Chance, you can't date her," I heard Devon say behind me.

I whirled around and stepped into him, drawing myself to full height even though I still stood two inches shorter than him. He needed to know he didn't intimidate me. "Why the fuck are you here, old man?"

The seriousness on his face melted into amusement, and he scoffed, "Careful, son. Rylee is only a year younger than me. You gonna call her old too?"

"I'm only going to ask you once more to tell me why you're here." I flexed my fists at my side as I stared him down. Red-hot rage boiled through my veins as I thought about how he'd fucked up my day in a matter of minutes.

We didn't do family visits. He'd never been a big part of my life. By the time he finally came around, I was fifteen and didn't care for anything he had to say. He'd been at my graduation, but we hadn't spoken. He finally gave up when I moved away from the town I grew up in and headed to Jacksonville. I was honestly surprised he was here since it was a little over an hour's drive from Sandridge.

He looked like he wanted to continue arguing but ultimately decided against it as he finally answered me. "Your grandparents are having their fiftieth-anniversary party in a few weeks. They'd like it if you came. I know you don't think much of me, but they've always been there for you. Even when Claire kept you away from them."

"My grandmother didn't keep me away from them. I chose not to see them that often so I wouldn't have to see *you*. A phone call would have been just fine, but you can tell them I'll think about it. Now leave, so I can go find my girlfriend."

I watched as his face went from relaxed to tight with anger again. "How long have you been seeing her?"

"My relationship is none of your business. But for your information, *dad,* I was the one who went after her. And I'll be damned if you think you're going to waltz into my life like you're a part of it and fuck up the best thing that's ever happened to me."

He had the audacity to chuckle lowly as he stared down at me and shook his head. "Oh, Rylee really did a number on you. She's beautiful, isn't she? You know, I don't think she ever really got over what happened between us. She made her entire family move to a different town so that she didn't have to see me anymore. But judging by how she looked at me when she opened the door, I could tell I still have an affect on her."

I took a step back and shook my head at him. "Yeah, she told me how she got her heart broken in high school. And about how she's never taken a chance on a relationship since then because of what you did. Until me. So, excuse me if I don't want to stand around wasting time measuring dick sizes. Because I think it's clear whose is bigger. Now please get out of my house."

DEVON HAD LEFT without so much as another word, and after driving to her apartment and not finding her there, I tried the only other place I could think of where Rylee would have run off to.

The bright neon sign for Sugar and Scotch was

turned off, and the lights inside were dimmed. I pulled around to the back, where Rylee's red Malibu was parked next to the fence, which reminded me to tell Tom that it needed to be replaced since the last storm had ripped it loose from the ground.

I had told Rylee multiple times that if she was going to be here alone, she needed to lock the back door, but a simple tug on it let me know she still wasn't taking that advice. Music blasted down the hall that led to the kitchen. Her purse and keys were thrown erratically on her office desk with its door wide open.

My steps were slow, and I shoved my hands in my pockets as I made my way closer to the racket of banging pans. I could hear her mumbling to herself, most of it incoherent, but I did pick up certain words like my name and Devon's name and '*stupid, foolish idiot*'.

Nervousness settled in my chest as I realized I had no idea what I would say to her. I didn't even know how *I* felt about the situation. What do you do when you find out your girlfriend used to bang your dad in high school? Age didn't matter to me, but even I couldn't deny, now that it had been thrown in my face, the fact that Rylee was the same age as my mother would be if she were still alive.

That wasn't the part that bothered me, though. It was the fact that I now knew that the great love my grandmother told me was my father's—before he knocked up my mom—was Rylee.

I couldn't even imagine the possibility of them being together. It made me physically ill. But it had happened once upon a time, and I could only guess what Rylee was feeling now. She already spooked too easily when it came to relationships. And regardless of the bomb that had gone off in my house thirty minutes ago, I still hoped she wanted to continue ours.

I interrupted her mumbling as I crossed my arms and leaned against the wall at the mouth of the entrance. "I keep telling you to lock that back door when you're here alone, Rylee."

She spun around, startled by my presence for the second time that day. "What are you doing here? You shouldn't be here," she spoke quietly. She sounded defeated—tired and annoyed that I'd encroached on her space.

I frowned as I registered that her words were a good indicator that this conversation would not go the way I wanted. "Listen, I know that you are probably panicking right now. I'm fully aware of the position we've just found ourselves in. But we need to talk about it, Ry."

She dropped her elbows to the large prepping table in the middle of the room and ran her hands up her face and through her hair to grip it at the roots. "Chance, I don't even know what to say to you right now. I don't know whether to feel ashamed or disgusted with myself. Or-"

"Whoa, whoa, whoa, Rylee. This doesn't change

anything. Not for me. You have to know that." I pushed off the wall and came around the table to pull her into my arms, but she twisted away and held up a hand, signaling for me to stay away. It stung, and I felt the sting of rejection throughout my whole body.

"This changes everything!" she cried out as she wrapped her arms around herself.

Tears slowly trickled down her cheeks, and I wanted nothing more than to reach out and wipe them away. To pull her into my arms and tell her it was going to be okay. But I stood there feeling completely helpless instead, respecting that she wanted some distance between us.

"Why does it have to change anything, Rylee? I don't have a relationship with him. As far as I'm concerned, Collin is my dad. Just like I call Claire mom. Devon has never been a part of my life-"

"But he was a huge part of *mine*! Chance, you don't get it. We grew up together. We were best friends before we started dating. In another life, he would have shown me your baby photos. I would have watched you grow up if he and I had made different choices. I could have been your stepmother!" she cried out, near hysteria.

A chuckle escaped from between my lips before I could stop it. "I don't know. I think that's kinda hot."

She didn't look amused, and I looked down at the floor as I quietly said, "Sorry."

"Can you take this seriously, please? You probably can't even begin to understand how much this is fucking with my head right now."

At least she wasn't crying anymore. She was angry. Angry, I could handle. "Yes, Rylee. Because finding out that my father dated my girlfriend while they were in high school and that he probably would have married her if he hadn't fucked up and had me isn't a huge fucking shock. What a huge mistake I must have been for your planned out perfect life."

She had told me all about how she and her ex had planned their lives together. Kids, a dog, a house with a white picket fence—which was why she'd been so hurt by what he had done. But now that I knew that it was my father who did it to her....

I wondered if she resented me even a little bit.

That thought sent a spear of pain lancing through my chest.

Rylee stared at me like I had physically hit her. But a moment later, her features softened, and she rushed forward to wrap her arms around me. I clung to her and buried my face in her neck, holding her like she'd disappear if I loosened my grip.

"You weren't a mistake, Chance. That isn't what I meant. I just.... I just need a little time to sort this out," she spoke against my skin before pressing a chaste kiss right below my jaw and then stepping back.

"If you want time, I can give you time." My voice sounded shaky, even to my ears. Tense waves rolled through my body like it was going into fight-or-flight mode.

But I would always fight for her.

"I'll give you all of the time you need. Because I know this shit is fucking weird. But what I won't do is walk away, not knowing if this will be the last time I see you. This isn't over. *We* aren't over. You're mine, Rylee. And I'm yours. So, I will give you all the time you need. But just remember, you're still my girl."

I stepped closer to her and wrapped my hand around the back of her neck, slowly drawing her in as I kissed her forehead lightly. And then, without another word, I dropped my hand and walked past her to leave.

Another storm looked like it was moving in as I walked to my truck. Thunder rolled in the distance, and as the rain started to pour, I couldn't help but wonder if I was in over my head.

CHAPTER ELEVEN

"How long are you going to avoid him, Ry? It's been a week, and you haven't so much as called him." Sadie sipped her dirty martini across from me on her oversized plush white leather sectional.

I sighed and pulled my attention back to the window, staring at the waves that crashed against the shore below. Sadie's condo was nestled in the top left corner of her building, overlooking the white sand and turquoise waters. It was a two bedroom two bath that was only *slightly* larger than my one bedroom one bath, but I could have bought two houses with the money she had spent on her place.

It was the complete opposite of her penthouse in New York—white walls with the typical beachy vibe. Accents of sand and Caribbean blue littered the rooms with seashell ornamentations and sea glass wall art from local vendors.

Sadie always joked that she had two sides to her,

like Dr. Jekyll and Mr. Hyde. New York was her fashionista former model, sitting in the front row at fashion week, self. While down here, she was just her. Just Sadie. Happy and carefree.

I sipped my rosé and clutched one of her elaborate decorative pillows tighter. "He hasn't called me either, Sade."

"Can you blame him? He thinks you decided he isn't worth it," she chided, albeit affectionately.

"And how would you know that?" I asked with thinly veiled mischief. I watched as her cheeks turned as pink as the wine in my glass, and she gulped down the rest of her martini.

"How *is* Tyler doing?" I asked as I turned to give her my full attention. I had noticed them growing closer over the last few weeks. Sadie always seemed bummed out after coming home from New York, and Tyler's goofy nature made her smile more and more often, even if she didn't want to admit it.

"He might have stopped by the other night before closing. He mentioned Chance has been testy at work. I'm not sure you noticed, but they had one of the new guys take care of the hedges this week." She stood and walked over to the kitchen to make another martini. "Want me to top that off?"

My glass was still nearly half-full, but I drained it and stood to join her in the kitchen, taking a seat on one of the white leather stools at the breakfast bar. She reached out for my glass as I motioned to the bottle. "Just give me the whole thing."

"Have you heard from Devon at all?" she asked as she unscrewed the lid to the olive container.

"No, which I'm kind of surprised, to be honest." I took a long gulp of my wine, the coolness of the liquid turned warm in my belly, and I could feel my skin flush. I was on my second bottle and, no doubt would be staying the night at Sadie's.

"Did you want to hear from him?"

"Absolutely not. Talking to Devon would just make things more complicated. You should have seen the way he looked at me, Sadie. Like I was a monster, who had defiled his little boy."

"What if that's not how he feels? What if it's the opposite? You said he tried to see you multiple times after you left Sandridge. What if he's more upset that Devon Jr. is the one keeping your kitty cat warm at night?" she questioned as she poured an ungodly amount of olive juice into her St. Louis Tommy Martini Shaker from Scully and Scully.

I reached over and popped an olive into my mouth, making a face as the salty bitterness mixed unpleasantly with the semi-sweet taste of wine already on my palate. I chewed it awkwardly as I replied, "God, this whole thing is a mess. And you know what I really want? I want things to go back to how they were before Devon knocked on that damn door. Chance had just asked me to move in, Sadie. You know how much I value my space. But I was going to say yes!"

Sadie looked at me with as much surprise as I

felt. I blinked and took another gulp of wine before I softly repeated, "I was going to say yes."

My heart swelled, and I didn't know if it was in pain or elation. Chance had gotten me to open my heart up again. Why would I give that up? It had only been two months but.... Every kiss, every touch, every morning I woke up in his arms—it all felt as natural as breathing.

"Well, don't you think you have your answer then?" Sadie lilted through my thoughts.

"I'll call him tomorrow. I've had too much to drink tonight. We should talk when I have a clear-"

Sadie turned and dumped her glass out, olives and all, and grabbed her keys from the small dish at the end of the counter. "No, no, no. You're going now."

I glanced at the clock and set my glass down as she rounded the breakfast bar and pulled me off the stool. My rosé threatened to come back up as I shouted, "Sadie, it's almost one in the morning! He's probably sleeping."

"Or he's got a younger, hotter girl over who has just been itching to jump on that pony, so now that you've pulled your head out of your ass, we're going."

I froze. Chance had given me space all week—yes. But he hadn't even sent me a text or called. What if he *was* with someone else?

Sadie shook her head as she pulled me out of her condo and locked the door. She'd somehow grabbed my purse without me noticing and held out my lavender pumps as I stood there dumbfounded and barefoot in the hallway. "Come on, put your shoes on," she urged.

"Maybe I should call first. Or take a shot first. Can I take a shot first?" I dug my heels in as she started to pull me away, but to my surprise, she paused and gave me a sharp nod and went about unlocking the door again.

"Yeah, that honestly doesn't sound like a bad idea." She rushed back into her condo and grabbed the bottle of Grey Goose that was still sitting out without a cap. "Take a swig."

I did as she said and tipped my head back, grimacing as I chugged a mouthful straight from the bottle.

"Again. First one was for the nerves; the second is for courage."

One more mouthful.

"And one more for the road," she prompted as she reached out and tipped the bottom of the bottle back up to my mouth.

For a moment, I felt like I would be sick. But then a warm flush spread throughout my body and released all those happy endorphins, morphing into an instantaneous buzz that lit my body up.

I was supposed to be going to tell Chance that I wanted to be with him.

But maybe he wouldn't mind a little makeup sex first.

I LEANED my forehead against Sadie's back while she knocked on Chance's door again. "I swear to god, if that thing comes over here and tries to eat me, I'm going to have it turned into a purse," she grumbled.

Gary had been lounging in the driveway, our ever-faithful watchdog, and had scared the shit out of Sadie when she pulled in. He was on his usual side of the house, where the driveway met the yard, and it looked like he had no interest in either of us. But she was still on high alert and didn't appreciate that Chance was taking his sweet time answering the door.

My stomach rolled with queasiness. Those shots were the worst idea after I'd drunk nearly two bottles of wine to myself. My body felt clammy, and saliva kept trying to pool in my mouth like it did just before you were about to toss your cookies.

The light finally turned on above the door, and I groaned in relief while Sadie muttered, "About damn time."

Chance opened the door as I lifted my head off Sadie. He wasn't wearing a shirt, just gray sweatpants, and his hair was tousled like he'd been in bed. He looked at us in mild surprise through sleepy eyes before those amber orbs widened as he observed the state I was in.

"Rylee? Are you okay?" he asked.

My body wanted me to throw myself in his arms

while my mind kept chanting, '*Don't throw up. Don't throw up.*'

Sadie pulled me in front of her and pushed me across the threshold into Chance, who lifted his arms and caught me as I stumbled into his chest. "Rylee here needs to talk to you, but I may have plied her with wine and vodka, and now your talk might need to wait till morning. Have a good night!"

I turned to flip her off and yelled, "Fuck you, Sadie!"

"Love you too!" she replied as she got into her black Mazda MX-5 Miata and drove off, leaving me standing in the doorway with Chance.

He cleared his throat to get my attention, and I turned from where I was still watching Sadie drive away with my nerve to tell Chance how I felt. He looked at me expectantly and reached over my head to shut the door. I kicked off my shoes, threw my purse next to them, and started to walk down the hall to his bedroom.

"Where is my cat?" Lame. But now I was embarrassed and nervous and it's what came out of my mouth.

I could hear him chuckle behind me, and I huffed, annoyed that Sadie had just put me on the spot and left me. I continued into the bedroom with him tailing behind slowly. Domino was sprawled out on his usual cushion, but as soon as he saw me, he jumped up and meowed, happy to see me, or so I told myself.

Picking him up, I cuddled him to my chest while he rubbed his head against mine. "There's my boy."

"Traitor," Chance joked behind me. "Am I getting cuddles too? Or are you here to tell me it's over?"

The question had my stomach twisting again, and I let Domino down as I turned to face Chance. He'd gotten back into his bed, sans sweatpants, and my mouth went dry as I let my eyes wander.

Fuck, he was fine.

He'd pulled the dusty-blue flat sheet up over his legs haphazardly and watched me with a hardened look like he was bracing for me to say I was done.

"Do you really think Sadie would have just left me if that were the case?" I crawled onto the bed slowly, my white linen shorts riding up as my coral sleeveless top hung low, offering Chance a view of my lacy lavender bra.

He gulped, and I tracked his throat as it bobbed, licking my lips as I reached him and swung my legs over his. His hands grabbed me on either side of my hips and squeezed as if he were making sure I was real. I watched emotions play out on his face as he slowly ran his hands up my sides—uncertainty, fear of rejection, desire.

I reached up and pulled my top over my head, grinning down at him as a familiar blaze settled in my stomach. "I'm sorry it took me so long."

His hands were scalding on my skin, and I tipped my head back as he palmed my breasts through the lace and ran his thumbs over my hardened nipples, the material adding to the sensation.

Chance shut his eyes and took a deep breath before maneuvering me off him and getting off the bed, his erection prominent in his boxer briefs. He put his hands on his hips and looked everywhere but at me as he stated, "You're drunk, Rylee. I think maybe you should sleep it off, and we can talk in the morning."

"Are you serious?" Was he rejecting me? I came here, obviously to be with him, and he's going to say no? I clambered off the bed, my foot getting stuck in the sheet in the process, and I nearly face-planted, but Chance righted me with an *I told you so* look on his face.

I stood taller and craned my neck back to see him. "I'm throwing myself at you, *literally*, and you're telling me to sleep it off?"

That fire in my belly grew as Chance scratched the back of his head. He looked tired and not in the mood to deal with me. His silence irked me, and I spat, "Fine, whatever."

I moved to leave the bedroom so I could call Sadie and tell her to get her fucking ass back here and get me. Tears stung my eyes, and I hastily wiped them away before I felt a sharp tug around my middle. Chance spun me around to face him as the pressure from his arm caused that heat, which was not what I thought it was, by the way, to jump into my throat, and my body broke out in a cold sweat as

I doubled over and threw up on the cream tiled floor.

Right at Chance's feet.

I WOKE WITH A START. A nightmare, featuring Gary trying to eat Sadie's purse, fading as I remembered the events of the night before and where I was. The faint scent of bleach filled my nose, and my mouth tasted like a mix of bitter coffee and mint.

Chance had put me in the shower after I'd gotten sick all over his floor. I remembered him washing the vomit out of my hair and putting me in one of his shirts afterward. He had made me rinse my mouth out before handing me a cup of plain black coffee, saying it would help me sober up. Then he had me brush my teeth before we went to bed.

It had been as if *I* were twenty-five years old.

Shame coursed through me as I peeked over Chance's shoulder at the clock on his nightstand. It was only five in the morning, but I felt as if I'd had a good night's sleep rather than only a few hours.

I watched Chance's shoulder rise and fall with his even breathing. His back was to me, the duvet kicked down to the end of the bed, and the flat sheet covered us both to our hips. I admired the muscles in his back, wanting desperately to reach out and run my fingers down them.

The overwhelming feeling of wanting him, to

feel his skin on mine, had my thighs clenching as a warmth settled between them. I reached out and gingerly lifted the sheet from his skin, peeling it back little by little until it came to his thighs. He shifted, head still turned away from me, as he rolled to his back and bent the leg closest to me so that his knee pointed out like he was beckoning me to come take up the space he'd created between his legs.

I shifted closer, his shirt riding up my thighs as I moved to my knees and gently crawled between his. My fingers trailed slowly up his thighs till they reached the fly on his boxer briefs, and I reached inside to pull him out.

He wasn't fully flaccid, nor was he fully erect. He was somewhere in the middle and growing harder as I cupped him softly in my palm. Chance was bigger than the last few guys I had been with. Longer, thicker, and knew how to use it better, too. As I pumped him slowly, my fingers went from being able to touch to barely fitting around his girth as his cock rose to greet me.

Chance let out a soft groan, shifting his hips upward as he danced on that thin line between sleep and consciousness. I slid down, laying on my stomach between his open legs, perched on my fore-arms, before lowering my mouth to the crown of his cock.

I flicked my tongue against the slit, savoring the slightly salty burst of flavor that was just *him*. He sucked in a breath and jolted awake, looking down at me before he fell back to his pillow. "Shit, Rylee. What are you doing?"

I responded by taking as much of him as I could into my mouth, relishing in the harsh "Fuck" that came from him. His shaft was silky against my tongue, veins cording around it, developing more prominently as I worked him with my mouth.

He reached down and gathered my hair out of my face, our eyes locking as I bobbed up and down slowly, applying extra pressure when I got to the head. He tipped his head back and groaned, his other hand fisting in the sheet beside him. "Rylee-"

I made a popping sound as I lifted my head and told him, "I'm fine, Chance. Now shut up and enjoy coming down my throat like a good boy."

My hand twisted up and down his shaft, coated in my saliva, while the other grasped his thigh. His hand twisted tighter in my hair before he splayed his fingers out over my head and pushed down.

I opened wide over his cock again, running my tongue down to his base before taking him in my mouth again as I moved the hand on his shaft down to his balls and cupped them.

As I gently massaged them, his hand gently guided my head up and down on his dick, lifting his hips slightly with every stroke. I was soaked between my thighs, but this was about him. I wanted to make him feel as good as he always made me feel, and I hadn't gone down on him nearly as much as he went down on me.

I shifted, tensing as I moved my hand down to gather the wetness between my thighs before stroking him again, coating him with my essence. The taste of myself on him caused me to moan around him, and the vibration resulted in him jerking his hips up as he pushed down on my head harder.

I choked around him, tears gathering in my eyes as he hit the back of my throat and held me there, cutting off my air. Looking up at him, I silently let him know with my gaze that it was okay, before he finally released me, and I drew back gasping for air.

"You're going to look so perfect with my cum painted all over you," he let out in a hoarse whisper.

I hummed in agreement as I caressed his shaft with long licks of my tongue, circling it around the tip before enveloping him in my mouth and then withdrawing again. "Is that what you want? To paint my skin with your cum? Or do you want me to swallow you down and lick up every last drop?"

He didn't have time to answer before I was on him again, pulling a long string of curses from him. Chance still watched me as I worked his cock, his other hand rising to caress my cheek before cupping it to have a better hold so he could thrust up into my mouth. "I want to smear every inch of your skin with my cum so that you don't forget who you belong to, Rylee."

Chance started to fuck my face, using both hands to push my head farther down onto his cock to the point where I struggled not to gag. "I gave you your space, and you had your time. Now you're fucking *mine*, do you understand?"

Since I couldn't answer, I managed to nod my agreement as wet slurping sounds filled the room with a palpable urgency. Chance roared as I tightened my lips and sucked hard. His cock tensed in my mouth, and he let go of my cheek to grab it in his hand as he released my hair and pressed his hips into the bed.

I closed my eyes and opened my mouth as he came, hot spurts of his cum coating my face and lips, and even my neck. I opened my eyes, thanking god he hadn't aimed there—I've had that happen, and it fucking stings—to see him staring at me, pride shining in his gaze.

"Fucking, look at you," he murmured, slowly continuing to stroke his cock until, at last, he was spent.

He grabbed the sheet that had been thrown aside and wiped my face. "I think I got your hair," he apologized with a smile before grabbing my chin and kissing me firmly. There was something so hot about a guy doing that after his dick had just been in your mouth.

"I've heard it's good for the skin, so, you know. Don't worry," I joked after he pulled back. Rising to my knees, I gathered the sheet to toss in the laundry basket and headed to the bathroom to clean up.

Chance watched me go, and I thought he might

join me, but he settled back against his pillows and was asleep again when I emerged from my third shower in twenty-four hours.

So, after I brushed my teeth once more, I grabbed a new shirt to sleep in from his dresser and crawled back into bed, wrapping myself around him and smiling as I fell back to sleep on his chest.

"TIME TO WAKE UP, BABY."

I groaned as Chance's voice filled my ear, still husky with sleep. "No, it's not morning yet."

He chuckled as I wrapped my arms tighter around my pillow and turned onto my side, squirming away from him a few inches. I cracked an eye open to see buttery sunlight filtering in through the gap in the curtains, and I gripped the duvet closer to my chest in denial.

Beneath the blanket, Chance ran his fingers along my thigh, and under the shirt I was wearing. His open palm moved slowly across my stomach, up the left side of my rib cage, until he reached my breast. He started to massage it, winding his other arm underneath my pillow and around my shoulders.

I let out a soft moan as he flicked my nipple with his thumb, drawing me back against his chest. My shirt rode higher, and I sat up quickly to remove it before Chance pulled me back down with my back to him. I hadn't put any underwear on after my shower, and my arousal pooled between my thighs as he nuzzled my neck, lazily nipping and sucking along my skin.

The arm underneath me wound its way across my chest to take over for the other as Chance dragged it back down my skin and between my legs. I sucked in a breath as he used two fingers to gather my arousal and spread it on my clit, swirling them around a few times before he plunged them deep into me.

I arched my back and cried out as he pinched my nipple and twisted it in time with the thrusting of his fingers. My hips rolled back against him, and the feeling of his rock-hard cock against my thighs had me spreading my legs so he could settle between them.

The air conditioning hadn't kicked on yet, and the air in the room was heavy and sticky, laced with the faint aroma of the citrus shampoo I had used in the shower just a few hours before, and sex. The only sounds were our heavy breathing and the wet sloppy noise of his fingers slipping in and out of me.

Sometimes words weren't needed in the early morning hours when you could just enjoy each other's bodies.

I lifted my leg and kicked it back to hook over his hip, half laying on my back as he groaned in satisfaction. Baring myself to him made me feel sexy and powerful, and I reached around to grab his neck and pull him in for a kiss. They were slow and deliberate, like the ones he had been leaving on my neck.

Chance removed his fingers, and I made a sound of protest but then felt the head of his cock as it nudged against my entrance, slipping up through my center once...twice...three times before he finally buried himself to the hilt inside of me.

I let out a cry of pleasure and threw my head back as he started to move within me, stretching me and making me feel deliciously full. His hand moved back to rub against my clit. His mouth pressed kisses into my shoulder and the length of my neck, up to the space below my ear.

I still held on to the back of his neck as his other hand continued to caress my breast, alternating between massaging it and twisting and pulling at my nipple. His thrusts picked up speed as he lightly scraped his teeth down my neck. Our bodies were covered in a sheen of sweat, and I loved how messy it all was.

"Fuck, baby, I'm about to come," Chance rasped against my shoulder.

The wet sounds we created as our hips smacked together, paired with my cries of pleasure and Chance's low grunts, created a euphoric symphony. His fingers moved faster and harder against my clit as he pounded into me from behind for a few more seconds until he came hard, sinking his teeth into my shoulder.

I could feel his cock twitching inside me as he

continued to come, and he pinched my clit and started to work it furiously between his fingers. That, coupled with the feeling of his teeth in my skin, tore my orgasm from me, and I clenched my inner walls causing Chance to release my shoulder to whisper in my ear, "Fuck yeah, baby."

"Yeah?" I moaned as I continued to move against him.

"God, yes." He continued to rub my clit between his fingers and pump into me, the intense feeling of ecstasy never stopping, and a few seconds later, I was coming again, my nails digging into his neck so hard I was sure I broke skin.

"Fuck, I love watching you come. The sounds you make. The way your face looks. It's my favorite fucking thing in the whole damn world," he whispered against my skin before capturing my lips in a kiss.

I sighed in contentment. I had missed this. I had missed *him*.

Our bodies moved slower and slower as our tongues melded together. When he finally pulled back, he nudged my nose with his and grinned at me. "Shower number four?"

CHAPTER TWELVE

WHEN I HEARD BANGING ON MY DOOR LAST night, an intoxicated Rylee was not who I expected. To be honest, I thought it was Tyler on one of his rants about how Sadie wanted him, but she wouldn't admit it.

So, when Sadie had pushed a drunk Rylee into the house and taken off, I wasn't exactly sure what to think. She could have just been there for drunk break-up sex, for all I knew. But the moment she went in search of Domino and asked where *her* cat was, I knew she was there to stay.

I just wanted to hear her *say* it.

"Mmmm. Something smells good. What are you making?" Rylee asked behind me as she came into the kitchen.

I looked over my shoulder to see that she'd dressed in her clothes from last night. Her hair was still slightly damp from the shower, towel dried and left in her natural waves. Her face was devoid of makeup, just a pretty flush from our morning activities.

I wanted to spend every morning like this.

"French toast and bacon," I replied after I looked back to the stove. I reached for my coffee cup and took a sip, savoring the bitter liquid as it flooded my veins with the rush I so desperately needed to have the conversation with her that I had been dreading. I needed to know where she stood. Even if she wanted to pretend like we hadn't just spent the week apart.

"I missed your cooking." She came and stood next to me, grabbing a mug from the cabinet and pouring herself a cup of coffee from the pot I'd made while she was in the shower. She went to the fridge, no doubt to grab the hazelnut creamer she poisoned her coffee with, and I snuck a glance at her to see her frowning as she searched it.

When her gaze cut to me, I shrugged and flipped the bacon. "I was a little mad after I left you at the bakery."

"So you took it out on my coffee creamer?" She sounded amused as she grabbed the milk and poured some into her cup before grabbing a spoon and the sugar container.

When she was done, she proceeded to her usual stool at the island, grabbing a piece of bacon on the way. "So, I know we need to talk about the elephant in the room."

I perked up a little, glad she was the one to say it first. "Yeah. I agree."

"What did your dad want?"

Yeah, that was not even remotely close to what I wanted to talk about.

"I'm more interested in why you showed up at my door last night drunk." I turned and handed her a plate with two pieces of French toast and some more bacon.

"You sound angry about that. You sure didn't seem to mind this morning. Or a few hours before that."

I turned around and shook my head. "Don't do that, Rylee. You don't get to act that way after you ignored me for a week."

She had the grace to look ashamed for a moment before she shrugged. "I thought you would be happy to see me."

"I was. I am. But I'm also confused. What does this mean? Was last night a one-time thing? Did you come here for breakup sex before you let me down?"

"What? Chance, no. I came because I realized our situation didn't matter to me. I wanted—I want—to work through it," Rylee exclaimed.

The beginning smell of burning bread filled my nose, and I turned to switch the burner off and move the pan to the back one before I braced my hands on the counter, my back still to Rylee.

I heard her push the stool back, and the soft steps of her bare feet on the tile before I felt her arms wrap around me from behind. I hung my head, and before I could stop myself, I asked, "Did you see him?"

"See who?" she sounded genuinely confused.

I sighed and turned in her arms, not embracing her back as I looked her dead in the eye and said, "My father. Apparently he stayed in town for a while. So, I'm going to ask you again. Did you see him?"

"No, Chance. I have nothing to say to Devon. I wouldn't have talked to him even if he had come to Sugar and Scotch. Look, I'm sorry I didn't say anything to you all week. But to be fair, you didn't say anything to me either." She went to pull away, but I locked my arms around her before she could move beyond my reach.

My heart hammered in my chest as I stared down at her. "You asked me for space and time, so that's what I gave you."

"Well, I don't want it anymore. I want you. I want us. And Domino and Gary. And, if you still want me to, I think I'd like to move in."

Adrenaline rushed through me like a dam that had burst. I beamed down at Rylee with a smile so large I thought my cheeks would split. "Yes. Of course, I still want that."

She stood on her tiptoes to give me a quick peck on the lips. "Well, then, I guess that's settled. We're together, and I'm moving in."

I remembered what Devon had said about my grandparents' anniversary party coming up, and as much as the timing was all wrong, I had already decided that I would be going. After all, they'd never done anything to me to deserve my ire. I didn't owe them anything, but the fact that they still thought to even invite me said a lot.

"Great, we can do it the weekend after next. After I get back from Sandridge."

I didn't miss the way Rylee froze as a look of puzzlement crossed her pretty features. "That's why Devon was here. To tell me that my grandparents wanted me to come to their fiftieth wedding anniversary."

Realization dawned, and she nodded her head slowly. I wouldn't ask her to go. The shock of seeing Devon would only be made worse if she had to continue seeing him. Paired with visiting my grandparents—it was too much to ask of her.

"Hey," she said softly as she reached up to cup my cheek. "I'll go. I want to be supportive of you."

I let out a short chuckle and asked, "Am I that obvious? I wasn't going to ask you, you know."

"I know. That's why I'm telling you I will go with you. I think it will be good for you to have a relationship with them, Chance."

"And what about our relationship? Are you going to tell them that you're dating their grandson now?"

She contemplated my question, and I watched it all play out on her face before she slowly nodded. "Yes. That's precisely what I'm going to tell them."

My heart burst with the fierce sensation of being

cared for–of being seen–by her. I'd never dated anyone who looked after me like I had them.

But in the short time we'd been together—and apart—Rylee already knew exactly what I needed.

CHAPTER THIRTEEN

Sandridge had changed. No longer the sleepy little town I grew up in, but instead, a larger, busier city. The hotel Chance had got us a room at was new, and none of the people that worked there were ones I recognized. I let out the breath I had been holding as Chance picked up our bags after we checked in and led me to the elevator that would take us up to our room.

Anxiety had my stomach tied in knots the whole drive there. Chance had been wonderful, continuously telling me that I didn't have to go if I didn't want to, and assuring me that we could leave at any time if I felt uncomfortable.

But I wanted to be there for him. I wanted him to know that I was all in. It was time to face my past and declare that Chance was my future.

I didn't really know at what point I had decided to let go of our age difference. And of the fact that

Chance was Devon's son. But sometime over the last two weeks, I realized that none of that mattered anymore.

Perhaps, it happened when I showed up at his house one afternoon and caught him dancing around the kitchen with Domino in his arms. Or when he politely but firmly told a girl his age he was taken when she hit on him at Sugar and Scotch–making a huge deal that it was me he was taken by. It could have even happened when he built an awning on the side of the house that Gary always chilled on so that he *'didn't have to sit in the rain while he hung out with Domino.'*

All I knew was that I was falling for him, and I was falling *hard*. Age difference be damned.

"What time is dinner at your grandparents?" I asked as we walked into our room.

It was big for a standard hotel room, with two queen beds and a small sitting area on the far side by a large window overlooking a picturesque courtyard with benches and small tables. The bathroom had a large double sink vanity and both a soaking tub and a walk-in shower. The room was decorated in cream with beige and black accents. Two prints hung on the wall, one above each bed, of a seagull on the beach looking out at the water and dune grass on a sandy knoll that looked like it was blowing in the wind, respectively.

"Six," Chance replied as he threw our bags on one of the beds. I opened the door to the closet, where I found hangers and an ironing board, and hung up my dress and Chance's suit for the party tomorrow.

As soon as I closed the door, I felt Chance's arms circle me from behind as he pressed a chaste kiss to the side of my neck. "It's only four-thirty. We have plenty of time to take a walk down on the beach if you'd like? Or you could let me ease some of this tension you're carrying. You're stiff as a board, babe."

His hands skimmed up my arms to settle on my shoulders as he started to rub and squeeze the knots that had settled there. I rolled my head forward and moaned. "That feels amazing."

"Come here. I'll give you a massage." He grabbed my hand and pulled me over to the bed that didn't have our bags on it. "Take off your clothes and lay down."

I laughed and put my hands on my hips. "And just why do I need to take off my clothes? You know damn well what's going to happen if I do."

Chance had been insatiable lately, fitting in sex wherever and whenever we could. No place had been off-limits, from doing it in his truck at the beach to the kitchen at the bakery. I'd kept telling him if we had spent all of that time moving my stuff into his house instead of having sex, then I would have been completely moved in by now.

Chance waggled his eyebrows at me as he reached for the hem of my yellow sundress. "That's kind of my point."

He captured my lips in a searing kiss as he slowly lifted my dress up my body before pulling back to drag it over my head. "On the bed, on your stomach." His tone was thick with anticipation as his eyes roamed down my body.

I raised an eyebrow at him and gave him a saucy smirk as I slowly turned and got on the bed, making sure to provide him with a show of my nearly naked body. He hadn't told me to remove my bra or underwear, and the cream-colored satin set stood out brightly against my tanned skin.

I let out a little yelp as he slapped one side of my butt before grabbing me by the calves and pulling my legs straight which caused me to fall face-first onto the bed. He chuckled as I picked my head up and whipped it around to glare at him.

Making a circling motion with his finger for me to turn around, he said, "Are you going to be a good girl and listen to me, or am I going to have to punish you?"

"Depends on what the punishment is," I muttered as I gathered my hair to the side and then folded my arms beneath me so I could rest my chin on them. "Remind me why I had to take my dress off again?"

He spanked me again, this time softer before I felt him get on the bed and straddle my thighs.

"So I can enjoy the view while I work," Chance replied. I heard him squirt something into his hands and rub them together to warm it up, and I wondered when he'd had time to grab whatever it was he was about to spread on my body.

The scent of cocoa butter filled my nose just before Chance's hands found my shoulders again and began working out the knots. I sighed, content, and closed my eyes, turning my head to the side to press my cheek against my folded arms.

He worked on my shoulders for what seemed like forever until the knots finally eased up, and then moved lower down my body. His hands were warm as they glided against my skin, down the sides and back up as he pulled and pressed his skilled fingers into my flesh. He'd barely skimmed the sides of my breasts before he then pulled his fingers down to my hips in long strokes.

He worked the sides of my hips before rolling his hands to my lower back, splaying his hands on either side of my body as he worked the muscles with his thumbs. With each stroke, the fingers that gripped me moved inward until he rubbed along the crease between my thigh and my pelvis.

My breath stuttered as he started to move slower, his pointer and middle finger on both hands slipping into my underwear to move just slightly closer to my aching center. I could feel his cock through his board shorts as it grew hard against the back of my thighs, and I shifted a little, pushing my butt up to create more room for his fingers.

"Ah, ah, ah. Patience, baby," he warned in a gravelly tone. I felt the pressure of him lift off me and settle at my side, his hands retreating to move lower down my butt as he palmed both cheeks with his hands, spreading them wide with every pass.

I squirmed against the bed, desperate for some sort of friction against my clit. Arousal pooled in my underwear, the wet satin sure to leave a spot that would be visible to Chance. He continued to work his way down to the tops of my thighs before his thumbs took over what his fingers had been doing–rubbing along the crease of my thighs until he moved them ever so lightly over my underwear, right where the wet spot was.

"Chance," I let out a low whine and arched my back, pushing my ass higher in the air.

He didn't say anything as he reached up to grab the satin straps of my underwear and pulled them down in an agonizingly slow manner. Once he'd peeled them down my legs, he ran his hands back up my thighs. One hand palmed one of my cheeks while the other slid between my legs and grabbed a handful of the tender flesh on the inside of my thigh.

It was almost painful how he handled me there before moving to the other side to do the same. My breathing was shallow as I gripped the plush blanket underneath me, my eyes still screwed tightly shut.

Finally, he cupped between my legs, using three fingers to run from my clit to my opening before he pushed all of them inside at once. I sucked in a breath and bucked sharply against the bed, undulating my hips in time with his slow rhythmic thrusts.

The angle of his fingers changed, stretching me wide as I felt him lay a kiss on the back of my neck as he picked up the pace, his thumb finding its way between my cheeks to settle at the puckered part of me I hadn't ever let anyone touch.

Chance had once told me he wanted to fuck me in the ass, but we had yet to do it. And as he moved his thumb down to collect some of the wetness that dripped out of me, when he pushed against that forbidden area again, I bit my lip hard as his thumb stretched me ever so slowly, just the smallest amount.

He didn't push his luck, just continued to work me slowly, never going past a certain point while his fingers were knuckle deep inside my pussy, curling against and stroking my inner walls. I didn't hate it. In fact, the sensation was driving me wild as I ground into the bed beneath me.

I flipped my head to the other side and opened my eyes to look back at him. He was staring intensely where his fingers kept disappearing inside me, his other hand stroking his cock that he'd pulled out of his shorts. The view caused another wave of arousal to stream out of me.

"Take them off, Chance. Fuck me, please. I want to feel you inside of me," I whined.

There was something about the way he shook his head, never removing his gaze from what he was doing when he answered, "No fucking way. I'm going to watch you come all over my fingers, and then I'm going to come all over this pretty fucking pussy. And when we get home Sunday, I'll finally claim this ass."

He let go of himself to slap my cheek again before using his hand to guide my hips up a little more, his thumb pushing in a little deeper before he gripped himself and continued pumping his cock in time with his fingers.

I had no choice but to lay there and watch while he made a fucking mess out of me, my clit begging for friction. I reached down and started to rub myself, letting out a whoosh of breath at his strangled moan and the slapping sounds of him working himself as he pounded into me with his fingers.

The feeling of it all was almost too much. So much pleasure coursed through my veins, dancing on the edge of my orgasm. "Spread your legs a little wider," I heard him command.

I did as he said, feeling like a dirty slut and loving every minute of it. I liked being bared for him to see me at my most intimate. I could only imagine the image of my pussy speared wide on his fingers, his thumb partially in my asshole as I rubbed my clit furiously.

The thought of it, of Chance getting off to it, gave me a boost of confidence, and I pushed my upper body down into the bed so he could get a better view, and I slapped my clit hard.

"Fuck, do that again."

I could tell he was close and holding back to

prolong the show, and I slapped my clit again, cliciting a sharp cry from myself as my orgasm hit me suddenly, and I came so hard I saw stars. It was only moments before Chance came with a strangled moan, and I felt his weight on my back and the hot spurts of his cum against my clit.

Breathing heavily, he slumped over me, bracing his weight on his forearms and knees. I felt him press an open-mouthed kiss to my side before he rolled onto his back. "God, you are incredible."

I turned on my side as I smiled over at him, half hiding my face in the blanket. "I didn't hate it."

He looked at me, brow furrowed in confusion. "Didn't hate what?"

I felt a blush break out on my cheeks as I answered, "You watching. Or your thumb. I liked it more than I thought I would."

His answering smile was breathtaking as he quickly positioned himself over me, knocking me back to the bed and capturing my lips with his own. I drew my knees up to either side of his hips and reached down to pull his shirt up as our tongues tangled and our bodies grew ready for round two.

We had more than enough time.

WE WERE TEN MINUTES LATE.

I gripped Chance's hand tightly as we walked up the bleached pavers to the door. My childhood home loomed just beyond the edge of the yard where Devon and I used to run around. Both houses stood the same as they had twenty-five years ago—one-story, green-painted concrete block with gray asphalt shingle roofing. Devon's parents, George and Lynette, had never moved, and the sense of familiarity didn't comfort me. Instead, it weighed heavily on my chest.

But I kept walking.

Past the vinca and petunias Lynette and my mother planted when I was barely a year old. Past the gerbera daisies Devon and I had tended to when we were younger–my favorite flower. Up the steps lined with potted asters to the same dark brown door I'd walked through a million times before.

I nervously smoothed down my dress and patted my hair as Chance drew me closer and placed a kiss on my temple. "You look gorgeous. Don't be nervous. The worst they can do is get upset, and then we'll leave. We don't owe them anything, okay?"

I took a deep breath and nodded as Chance reached forward to push the doorbell. Barely a few seconds went by before the door opened wide to reveal Lynette. She was dressed in a smart peach pantsuit, her natural gray bob perfectly coiffed, with a string of pearls around her neck.

She broke out in a huge smile and held open her arms. "Chance! It's been too long. Come give your grandma a hug."

Chance stepped forward and embraced her, and

I noticed his body was as tense as mine. He'd changed into a black button-up and a pair of slacks, so I'd assumed that he must have spent at least enough time with the Eddisons when he was younger to know that a casual dinner meant business casual clothing.

She cupped his cheeks as he pulled back and looked at him with pure adoration in her eyes. "I missed you, my handsome grandson. I wish you'd come to visit more often."

Her gaze turned to me, and I froze, unsure of what to do or say. But not even a second passed before she gathered me in her arms and squeezed me tightly. "Rylee Raye Remmerson. I thought I'd never see you again, dear child. When Devon told us the news, I almost died of shock. You sure have a way with our Eddison men, don't you, my dear?"

I let out the breath I'd been holding and hugged her back as my sinuses burned from unshed tears. "Lynette. I know it's been a long time. You're not upset?"

She pulled back and looked at me in astonishment. "Why? Because of your age difference? Heavens no. There are ten years between Georgie and myself. Age is just a number, dear. If you make our Chance happy, and he makes you happy, then that's all that matters to us. Devon was an absolute fool to let you go so easily after you left. But fate brought you back to us. You were always meant to be part of this family, Rylee. Devon will just have to find a way to deal with it."

Lynette turned and motioned for us to come into the house. "Come on now. I just finished the salad, and Georgie is finishing up the steaks on the grill out back. Rylee, help me set the table so we can catch up."

Chance and I shared a glance before we both smiled, and I followed her while he made his way down the hall to the open door that led to the back patio. I could hear George's loud, jovial greeting, which made me smile as I went to the china cabinet, still in the same place it had always been, to grab plates and glasses for the table. It was a chore I'd done multiple times in the past, and Lynette resumed her post in the kitchen, where it looked like she had been making fresh lemonade when we had arrived.

"You know, Rylee. I told Devon not to surprise Chance the way he did. I told him there was nothing wrong with me giving him a phone call and asking him to come down for the party. But I do feel that he would have said no if it weren't for you." She spoke while she cut up lemons.

"They have a pretty complicated relationship, don't they?"

She snorted. "Complicated doesn't even begin to describe it. I love my son, I do. But we both know he is not without his faults. He is in his forties and still acting out like a child when he doesn't get what he

146

wants. He did it when you left. He did it when Chance was born. When he finally got his life together and returned home, he thought everything would be okay, and everyone would just accept his choices. But no one was about to force Chance to accept that his father had been absent his whole life, and Devon didn't know the first thing about being a dad. Poor Georgie felt like he'd failed him. Claire and Collin almost filed a restraining order against Devon because he wouldn't leave them alone. After that, Chance barely came around–not that he was around much to begin with.

"Devon had a way of popping up randomly every now and then. He always treated Chance as though he were competition, not family. Certainly not like he was his *son*. And we wanted to see Chance, but we weren't going to fight Claire. He was all she had after she lost Cherie, at least until they found Collin. Had she stayed with that miserable bastard she had been married to before, we would have fought tooth and nail to keep Chance out of that home. But she wisened up and left immediately. And she always kept us in the loop about where they were and how Chance was, and for that, we will always be grateful."

Her story filled my heart with sorrow for everyone involved. What a life that must have been for all of them. It hurt my heart to hear that Devon had never learned to be a good father. Chance had always told me he had a strained relationship with his dad and that he never saw it getting any better. I couldn't imagine not having a relationship with my parents, but I was also blessed with a wonderful mother and father.

Which reminded me.

"I'm sorry for the way things happened, Lynette. For asking my parents to move us away. I asked them to cut off all communication with you and George. It was a childish thing to do, and I know they did it because they love me. But now that I'm older, I can't imagine my best friend abandoning me over something that happened between our kids."

I joined her in the kitchen, and my muscle memory kicked into gear as I flitted about to gather the silverware and a bowl for the salad that lay deconstructed on various cutting boards on the counter.

"It was unfortunate, but I do understand where they were coming from. I'm going out on a limb here but I'll bet your mother hasn't ever told you that we actually kept in touch. They'd be coming tomorrow if they weren't on that cruise."

I was shell-shocked for a moment that my mother had indeed kept that from me, and that I'd come close to having her and my dad find out about Chance and I if they would have been at the party tomorrow. But I was glad to know that their friendship had survived. I would have to ask her why she never told me, even in the last few years, that she had stayed in touch with her friend. And I would need to come clean about who Chance really was before they heard it from anyone else.

"Where's my girlie?!" George's loud voice filled the kitchen, and I turned to see him coming at me with his arms wide open. He crushed me in a bear hug and then pulled back to ruffle my hair, something he'd done my entire childhood. He was dressed in gray slacks and a tucked-in peach button-up to match Lynette's suit. It warmed my heart to see them still so happy after all these years.

"Hi, George." I smiled warmly at him.

"Still just as pretty as the last day we saw you. Our Chance is a lucky man," George said affectionately before he went and kissed Lynette on the cheek.

"Don't I know it," Chance said from where he'd been standing behind George. He set the plate of steaks he was holding down in the center of the table before he walked over to my side and put an arm around my waist, drawing me into him.

"Everything okay in here?" he whispered in my ear under the guise of kissing the side of my head.

I gave him a reassuring nod and squeezed the hand that was settled on my waist. He'd gone through so much. Their whole family had. A lot of it because of me. I felt guilty, but at the same time I also felt selfish because Chance had turned out so wonderful and I was thankful things had turned out the way they had.

As we all settled around the table and Chance

started answering their questions about how life was in Jacksonville and how his business was going, I took it all in with a happy heart. Dinner passed with friendly conversation as we all caught up with each other, and I was elated that I had decided to come with Chance.

I made a mental note to call my parents and fill them in on everything so they could perhaps stop hiding their friendship with Lynette and George. The Eddisons had deserved better, but they were still the kind and forgiving people that they had always been my whole life.

The night grew dark as dinner turned into dessert: Lynette's famous banana cream pie. Chance held my hand under the table, running his thumb across mine, while George dished up vanilla ice cream and Lynette served the pie.

Just as I took my first heavenly bite, the sound of the door opening had every member at the table freezing in place.

Steps sounded down the hall, growing closer and closer until Devon turned the corner, twirling his keys around his finger. Chance gripped his fork so hard I thought he might bend it while Lynette shot her son a look that said *what do you think you're doing?*

"Well, well, well. Aren't we just the happy little family? Thanks for the invite, Mother. I happened to see Chance's truck on the way home and figured I'd stop in," he drawled.

His eyes locked onto mine, and I found myself unable to look away from his hardened stare. Chance's hand found mine again as he picked it up and entwined them on the table. I pulled my eyes away from Devon to stare at our hands, then over to Chance, who had leaned back in his chair as he glared at his father.

"I'm surprised to see you here, Rylee. I didn't expect you'd be coming," Devon snarked.

My eyes found his again, but he was staring at Chance's and my joined hands. "Why wouldn't I be here?"

Lynette picked up the wooden spoon from the salad bowl and shook it at her son. "Devon, beat it. You know exactly why you weren't invited to dinner tonight. Go on next door, and I'll bring you over some pie when we're done. We're going to have a little chat."

"Next door?" my voice was small as I asked the question. Surely that didn't mean what I thought it did.

"Oh, they haven't told you yet? I bought your old house, Rylee." Devon looked at me smugly. "Had to do some repairs, though. The people that bought it from your parents never fixed the holes we put in the wall from your bed-"

Lynette smacked the wooden spoon on the table so hard it made me jump. "That is enough, young man! Go home! And you better be on your *best* behavior for the party tomorrow!"

Chance's grip on my hand bordered on painful, and though I'd just been dealt the blow that Devon now occupied my childhood home, I nudged his leg with mine to try and keep him from jumping up from the table and dealing Devon a punch to the face he so strongly deserved.

Devon let out a low chuckle and turned to leave. "Oh, I will, Mother. You know I would never do anything to ruin your party. You might want to tell your guests the same, though. You know the gossip mill will be turning tomorrow when my ex-girlfriend shows up on my son's arm."

He left without another word as I stared, dumbfounded, at the place that he had occupied. I hadn't even thought of that.

But it seemed as if Lynette had.

"Don't worry about it, dear," she said. "Who cares what anyone else has to say about your relationship? All that matters is that you two are happy."

George voiced his agreement before finally digging into his pie, a little less happy than he'd been before Devon's arrival. Chance pushed his plate away and gave Lynette a sad smile.

"I'm sorry, Grandma. But I've lost my appetite."

She nodded in understanding before she got up and grabbed some Tupperware. "I know the hotel has a mini fridge in the room. You can take yours to go. Rylee, I know you enjoy banana cream." Her voice was softer than it had been all evening, and I could tell she'd also been bothered by Devon's unannounced appearance.

I nodded, unsure what to say, so I just uttered a soft, "Thank you."

We quickly said our goodbyes and headed back to the hotel, both of us quiet during the drive.

But later that night, as we cuddled in bed wrapped in each other's arms, we agreed not to let what anyone said the next day bother us. After all, it wasn't like we planned to visit Sandridge often.

Lynette and George could visit us.

CHAPTER FOURTEEN

Rylee

THE SANDRIDGE COMMUNITY CENTER HAD BEEN decked out to the nines for the party. Flowers filled every table and extra space. Balloons littered the dance floor. And there was a giant backdrop of a photo of Lynette and George on their wedding day, with golden balloons attached that spelled out *Happy 50th Anniversary*.

By the time Chance and I had arrived, the main parking lot was full, and we had to park in the overflow lot half a block down. Chance looked dapper in a navy suit with a light blue button-up. I had chosen a mauve sheath dress with thin straps and beaded detailing along the top that trailed down and tapered off under my breasts. It hugged my curves and fell just above my knees with a small slit on one side.

Just before we had walked in, Chance grabbed my hand and kissed it. Then we opened the door and faced whatever we would find on the other side.

Lynette and George were quick to see us and raced over to say their hello's. They were both dressed in cream, her in a beautiful dress with lace overlay and him in a sharp suit with a navy bow tie.

It hadn't taken long for me to feel like someone was staring, that sense of awareness prickling along my skin, and it had taken even less time to find Devon's eyes across the room. He was dressed in a suit a deeper blue than Chance's with a white button-up that was open at the collar, and sipping what looked to be amber-colored liquid from what I could tell.

He raised his glass in our direction, and I shifted closer to Chance's side, raising an eyebrow as if to say *you can't bother me*.

Devon smirked as if we'd just shared our own private joke, and for a moment, I was transported to when we were teens. We'd been inseparable, and now we couldn't stand each other. And while I had spent most of my adult life running from relationships because I never again wanted to experience the hurt he'd put me through, I also had received the greatest happiness I had ever known from Devon–in Chance.

We grabbed glasses of champagne and made our rounds. Most of the faces I recognized from my youth and they all stared at me like they weren't sure what to think. It wasn't long before the whispers started, heads nodding in our direction and then over to Devon.

If Chance noticed it, he didn't say anything, but as Julie Peterson–Sandridge's biggest gossip and Lynette's frenemy–walked toward us through the crowd, I had a feeling that Chance was about to get it thrown right in his face.

"Rylee Remmerson! It's been so long! Look at you all grown up. You are just as pretty as a peach. And you must be Chance, Lynette's grandson. How sweet of you to accompany your stepmother. Your daddy looked like he was busy fighting off the whole garden club earlier. I'm sure you have your hands full with that one, don't you, Rylee?" she lilted in her syrupy sweet voice and grinned at us as she sipped her champagne.

Some things never changed.

Chance, to my surprise, laughed, and before I could respond to her, he jabbed, "I'm sorry, ma'am, you must be mistaken. Rylee and I are actually dating. I'm not sure what gave you a different impression."

She blinked, and I smiled as Chance held me tighter. "As a matter of fact, I haven't seen or even spoken to Devon until about three weeks ago. I think you're losing your touch, Julie. If you'll excuse us."

I reached out and gently touched her on the arm before Chance and I walked away, and I could only imagine that she was already off to spread the news and confirm what everyone else was already wondering.

Chance took my glass and set it on a nearby table

before he held a hand out and asked, "Dance with me?"

"Of course." I let him lead me onto the dance floor and pull me close as a slow song started. He rubbed small circles on my lower back, where his hand rested, as I played with the hair at the nape of his neck, and I knew we made quite the image.

"How are you doing?" he whispered, moving closer to rest his mouth close to my ear.

"I'm fine. It doesn't bother me as much as I thought it might. What about you?" I responded as I caught Devon's eye over Chance's shoulder.

He stood at the edge of the crowd that littered the area around the dance floor, watching us while other people in the room watched him. Lynette and George were only a few couples away from us, looking utterly in love, none of what was happening having an effect on them.

"Can I be honest?"

"Always." I pulled back to look him in the eyes and noticed that his smile had dropped.

"You used to love him, Rylee, and he knows it. He hates me. He hates us together. And I don't think he's going to stop trying to get a rise out of us. He hasn't taken his eyes off you since we walked in, and I'm seconds away from going over there and putting him in his place," Chance bit out.

I frowned and reached up to cup his cheek. "Loved, Chance. Past tense. When we were kids. And he doesn't hate you, you're his son. He just doesn't know how to be a good parent. He was so young-"

"And now you're making excuses for him?" Chance halted our dance, and his grip loosened around me.

I bristled, dropping my arms from his shoulders. "No, I'm not. I'm not saying that anything he's done is okay. But you need to be the bigger man, Chance. You're better than ruining your grandparents' party over something so petty."

He scoffed and backed up a step. "Do you love me, Rylee?"

His question caught me off guard, and the weight on my chest increased. "W-what? Chance, this isn't the time to have this conversation."

I had promised myself once upon a time that I wouldn't use that word ever again, not unless I really meant it. Did I love Chance? A large part of me wanted to say yes. But there was still a tiny part of me, as much as I hated to admit it, that wondered if we would last. Our age difference, and Devon, would always loom over us. Life together would always be somewhat difficult. Was I ready for that?

Was he?

He nodded and looked down at his shoes, "That's all I needed to hear, Rylee. Excuse me."

"Chance-" I started. But he walked off the dance floor before I could say anything else, and I didn't want to create more of a scene than we already were.

I found Devon's eyes again, like a beacon calling

to me. His expression wasn't smug but contempla-tive—like he'd just figured out part of a complicated puzzle. And just as he looked like he was about to step out toward me, I turned and headed to the bathroom.

I needed a little time to collect my thoughts.

DEVON, Chance, and I seemed to be all anyone could talk about. The bathroom had been filled with, '*I heard she's sleeping with both of them.*' And, '*She and Devon made the most handsome couple when they were younger. Can you imagine what their kids would have looked like?*'

The whispers followed me around the room, and if I had heard them, then it was likely that Chance had too. I had been occupied with numerous guests that recognized me from years ago, saying hello and trying to get the truth about what was really going on. He was currently continuing to ignore me as he danced with a bunch of little kids on the dance floor.

I wondered what his life would hold if we were to stay together. I didn't want to have children, and he said he didn't either but what if he changed his mind in a few years? It wasn't even something we had discussed since that night on the beach. I wasn't even sure I could have them at my age. When I entered menopause, Chance would be in his prime.

How was that fair?

As Chance danced with the little kids, entertaining them while their parents mingled, I sipped my champagne while my mind went down a rabbit hole of all of the ways I would fuck up his future.

"Hi, there," I heard from my left, stirring me from my thoughts.

I turned my head to see a beautiful brunette smiling at me. She had bright blue eyes and deep chocolate waves, and was wearing a dress that looked like it had been painted on her perfectly sculpted body.

"I'm Abigail." She offered her hand to me.

"Rylee," I said back as I reached out to shake it.

She turned her attention to Chance on the dance floor and sighed wistfully. "He's perfect, isn't he?"

My hackles raised like a dog with a bone. Instantly alert, my body went rigid as I gave a slight nod. "He is."

"We used to date, you know. I thought he was it for me, but then he went and had to move to Jacksonville. Said he was looking for something *more*. I didn't get it then, but now I do. He always had such an *old* soul," she said in a syrupy sweet lilt that had me wondering if she was related to Julie.

I clenched my jaw as she sighed again, and I was about to say something petty back when Devon appeared at my side with two glasses of champagne. I drained the glass I was holding and reached for the one he offered me as he gave Abigail one of his charming smiles.

"If you don't mind, I'm going to steal Rylee away real quick, Abby."

I wondered how he knew who she was and why she was even here in the first place. Chance hadn't grown up in Sandridge. And Devon hadn't been in Chance's life enough to know his girlfriends.

"Of course, Mr. Eddison! It was so lovely to meet you, Rylee." Abigail had the nerve to reach a hand out to lay on my arm before flipping her perfectly curled hair behind her and walking over to Chance.

I watched as she said hello, and how he awkwardly greeted her back as she stepped forward to kiss him on the cheek. She pulled his arms around her, forcing him into a dance, knowing that he would be polite and oblige her.

He didn't need my permission, but it stung that he didn't even look around for me.

"Dance with me," Devon's whispered words rang too close to my ear.

My head spun with a champagne buzz, and I raised my glass to drain it again when Devon reached out and took it from my grasp. "I think you need to slow down there, babe."

"I'm not your *babe*. What are you even doing, Devon? Do you want to explain to me why one of Chance's ex-girlfriends is here? She's towns away from where he grew up."

"I figured he could use a distraction while you and I talked. Come on." He wrapped an arm around my waist, and the weight of it was too heavy. It felt all wrong.

But Chance smiled at Abigail like he'd smiled at me earlier, which crushed my heart. Why would he choose to be with me when he could have her?

I swallowed the lump in my throat and allowed Devon to lead me into the dance, very aware that we had drawn the attention of a crowd of ladies who were cooing to each other about how it was inevitable that we would find our way back to one another.

That was the problem with small towns. No one knew when the fuck to move on.

"Do you really think you two are going to last?" Devon asked me. He was pressed too close to me, and instead of craning my neck to meet his eyes, I turned my head to the side.

And caught Chance's furious stare.

I ignored him. He didn't get to be mad at me when he had readily accepted Abigail's advances.

"I think you're with him because he reminds you of me," Devon continued softly. "But look at him with her. You're going to tell me you won't wonder if he's ever thinking about a younger woman? That you don't wonder if he will grow to resent you and eventually decide the age difference *does* matter?"

Tears stung my eyes, and my sinuses burned as I

held them back. I bit the inside of my cheek and looked up at him, and his eyes softened as they saw how glassy mine had become.

"Hurting you was the biggest mistake I ever made, Rylee."

"Don't," I interrupted him. "I don't want to hear that now, Devon."

"Then when? Give me an hour of your time. Have coffee with me. Let me explain-"

"There's nothing to explain," I whispered as a tear rolled down my cheek. I tucked my head into his chest so the other guests wouldn't see me cry, and I wondered what it looked like to Chance.

I wondered if he gripped Abigail's waist tightly as he watched us, and the thought had my fists clenching, inadvertently pulling Devon closer.

"Can we just let it all go, Devon? We used to be friends once upon a time. I don't think we will ever get that back, but we don't have to go out of our way to hurt each other."

"You think it doesn't hurt me to watch you with him? To know that my son is *fucking* the love of my life?" Devon whispered angrily.

I pulled back to look up at him with a look of disbelief painted on my face. "You don't *know* me, Devon. I'm not the love of your life. We aren't two stupid lovesick teenagers anymore."

I jerked out of his hold, no longer caring who was watching us. "You may think that hurting me was the biggest mistake you ever made, but one day you're going to wake up and realize that you've thrown away the greatest gift you've ever been given–*your son*. And the pain you think you feel now will be *nothing* compared to that one."

The crowd parted as I hastily moved through the room, and I was reminded that I would need to apologize to Lynette and George later for causing such a scene. Anger and frustration coursed through my veins as I stormed down a hall connected to the main room. I heard footsteps behind me and picked up my pace, assuming that Devon had followed me, and I didn't want to continue fighting with him.

Just as I passed an open door that looked like it was to some sort of storage room, a hand grabbed me by my arm from behind and hauled me into it. The door slammed behind me, and I spun to see Chance standing there as he breathed heavily.

It only took him two long strides before he pushed me back against a stack of storage bins and reached down to lift me by my thighs. My legs wrapped around his waist on instinct as he crushed his lips to mine. He balanced me on the bins as he pushed up my dress and yanked my underwear down, removing them before he shoved them in the pocket of his suit jacket.

I moaned against him as I tried to pull back and ask what he was doing. We were in a public place, with a room full of people mere feet away. But his lips abused mine, not letting up as he jerked the button on his pants open and tore the zipper down, pulling his cock through the fly on his boxer briefs.

He slid up through my center twice before he plunged into me. My walls clamped down around him, and he pushed in deeper, swallowing the noises I made as he started to pound into me at a punishing pace.

He released my lips with a sharp nip to my bottom one, before he growled, "I don't know what kind of game you think you're playing, Rylee, but I'm not interested. You said you were mine. So why the fuck did you look so comfortable in his arms?"

"Like you looked with Abigail?" I fired back before surging forward to claim his mouth. My hands were desperate to touch his skin, and I pushed his jacket from his shoulders and started to unbutton his shirt with urgency, running my hands across his chest and down his stomach when I got it open.

He broke our kiss and spat, "If you were jealous, you could have cut in."

He looked down to where we were joined, watching as he slid in and out of me, and I kept one hand on his shoulder while the other reached down and lifted my dress higher, giving him a better view. "You could have done the same."

His eyes locked on mine again, and the fire in them burned bright with something I couldn't place. His thrusts were erratic, and the angle caused my clit to rub against the fabric of his boxers. I threw my head back against the wall as he continued to punish me with his cock.

After a few more thrusts, I could feel my walls contract as I neared my climax. Chance must have felt it, too, because he picked up his pace and gripped me so hard that I would probably bruise.

As I came, I let out a loud moan, and he roared his release right behind me. As soon as he stopped twitching inside me, he pulled out and tucked himself away again as I reached for his jacket and fished out my underwear before handing it back to him.

"We need to talk about this," he said as he breathed heavily and buttoned his shirt back up.

I slipped my underwear back over my nude pumps and headed to the door. "I agree."

After checking that he was ready to leave the room, I smoothed my dress and hair and opened the door.

Only to find Devon on the other side.

He looked between us and shook his head as he settled his gaze on me. "Sex in public, Rylee? At my parents' anniversary, no less?"

"Shut the fuck up and don't talk to her," Chance told him; simultaneously, I shook my head and opened my mouth to deny that was what we had just done.

Why I had been about to lie, I hadn't a clue. It was a knee-jerk reaction to getting caught doing something I knew was wrong. The three of us had completely hijacked the Eddison's anniversary party.

"Don't try and deny it, Rylee," Devon purred as he leaned closer, fingering a lock of my hair, as he said loud enough for Chance to hear. "You forget I know what you sound like when you come."

I felt the air around my face stir as Chance flew past me, landing a fist straight into Devon's nose. I yelped and jumped back as Chance hit him again across the cheek. The noise caused a few people to look down the hallway, and I heard the shrill cries of women and the shouts of men for Chance to stop.

George rushed down the hall to pull Chance off Devon while Lynette, having pushed her way to the front of the crowd, watched on in horror. George helped Devon to his feet and led him away while telling the guests crowding the small hall to return to the party and that the show was over.

"What the hell is wrong with you?" I turned and yelled at Chance.

"I fucking hate him!" Chance roared. "And you know the worst part? The worst part is that it kills me that he knows what you feel like against his body. That he knows what you taste like. It fucking haunts me the way he looks at you. We should never have come here, and I'm sorry I brought you. I'm sorry for making a scene. But if I have to watch that prick touch you one more time, I will break his fucking hand, so help me god, Rylee."

"You're acting like a child, Chance." The

moment the words left my mouth, I knew they were the wrong ones. I sounded like a parent scolding their kid. And Chance was too engulfed in his anger to be rational at the moment.

His features tightened, and he nodded, looking down at the floor. Without another word, he made his way down the hall and through the party, multiple people turning to watch as he left before they turned to me with questioning looks.

Whispers broke out around the room, and I turned to see Devon holding a napkin full of what looked like ice against his cheek.

"You know, he thinks you hate him. He's never asked you for anything, Devon. He's your *son*, and all you've ever done is cause him heartache and grief. I think it's time for you to either make amends or let him go," I said softly.

I turned and followed the path Chance had taken through the crowd. People murmured in hushed tones all around me, but I couldn't bring myself to care what they said.

I walked toward the truck, where I assumed Chance was waiting. My steps were deliberate so that I could apologize as soon as possible. But as I turned the corner to the parking lot, I stopped short when I saw his truck was gone. Despair coursed through me as I pulled out my phone to call him, but after two rings, it went straight to voicemail.

My bottom lip trembled slightly as I debated going back into the party to hide until it was over and

I could catch a ride with George and Lynette. But I ordered a Lyft instead, to take me back to the hotel. It seemed as if I had finally pushed Chance to his breaking point. I only hoped I wasn't too late to make it all right.

CHAPTER FIFTEEN

Our hotel room was empty when I returned. There was no sign that Chance had been there since we'd left earlier that afternoon. It was nearing ten, and almost three hours had passed since Chance left me at the community center.

His phone kept ringing once or twice before going to voicemail, and eventually, I stopped calling as my anger took hold. I understood why Chance was upset, but I didn't understand how he could strand me and then not answer my calls.

That *was* childish.

For all I knew, he'd gone back to Jacksonville, though I believed even that was too extreme for him. I texted Sadie to fill her in, but she hadn't responded yet, and I assumed she was getting ready to close up Sugar and Scotch.

I'd walked down to the hotel bar, sitting by myself at a table against a window that overlooked the beach. The sun had set, making way for the stars to shine against the night sky, and the inside of the bar was aglow with the ambiance of a roaring fire and dimmed lighting.

The fire was a nice contrast to the cool air conditioning the hotel had been blasting earlier. And it would have been romantic under other circumstances.

I sipped a glass of rosé as my anxiety grew. It, paired with all the champagne I had at the party, was not a good combination with the uneasiness that settled in my stomach. I wasn't sure if the nausea I felt was from the alcohol mixing or the way my nerves were frayed with the tension of not knowing where Chance was.

As if the night couldn't possibly get worse, a familiar tingling sensation crept up my spine. I closed my eyes, knowing that when I opened them again, I would see the only person that I'd ever been *that* aware of his presence.

The sound of the chair across from me being pulled back forced me to open them. Devon sat there, nose slightly swollen, with a fresh bruise spread across his cheekbone. "Where's Chance?"

I sighed, leaned my elbows on the table, and put my head in my hands. "I don't know."

"He just left you here?" he sounded angry, and I knew he'd be even more furious when I told him the truth.

"No, he left me at the party. I took a Lyft here.

He won't answer my calls or texts. And I don't have his location, so I have no clue where he's at."

Devon clenched his jaw, and even with the bruise on his face, I had to admit he looked handsome. I'd always thought he was the hottest when he was heated about something. And I felt a stab of shame for even having the thought.

"What are you doing here?" I asked him, sitting back in my chair and picking up my glass. I didn't miss the way his eyes roamed down my body, and by the time he looked at my face again, I was giving him my best *eat your heart out* look.

"Looking for both of you. I think we all need to have a little talk." He sat back in his chair and held my gaze across the table.

Now that I had a moment to really look at him, I saw so much of Chance and wondered if this was always destined to be my fate–tied to Devon in one way or another.

I was about to open my mouth and say something witty, but my phone started buzzing in the middle of the table, and I lunged for it instead. Sadie's name popped up on the screen, and my shoulders sagged when I saw it wasn't Chance. But I pressed accept and held the phone up to my ear.

"Hey, Sade."

"Rylee! Oh my god, what is happening down there? I just read your messages. Where the fuck is Chance? Tyler said he's not answering his phone. And why the hell don't you guys just come home?"

She sounded like she had me on speakerphone, and I could hear the clinking of glasses in the background.

I ignored the look Devon was giving me and turned my gaze back out the window instead. Out of my peripheral, I did see him reach for my glass, and I didn't say anything as he took a drink.

"I have no idea where Chance is. He left me at the party, and I haven't seen him since. He won't pick up the phone for me either. I'm currently in the hotel bar, talking with Devon. Did you say Tyler was with you? Is he helping you close down the bar?" I asked slyly.

I could practically hear Sadie's eyes roll as she quipped, "Good puppies need to be continually trained."

"Hey!" I heard Tyler in the background, and it made me smile. He muttered something else I couldn't make out, and the phone sounded like it was changing hands.

"He's at a place called Butter Rum. It doesn't look like it's too far from the hotel you guys are at," Tyler's upbeat tone came over the line, and I realized I was no longer on speakerphone.

"It would figure that you'd have his location when I don't," I joked. I looked over to Devon, who was clearly waiting for me to tell him where his son was.

"Butter Rum?" I whispered.

He nodded and stood, motioning for me to get off the phone. I guess that meant he was driving, and we were both going. "Thanks, Tyler. I'm gonna head there now."

"Hey, Rylee? He's got daddy issues, if you haven't guessed that already. So this whole thing? It's been tough on him. I don't think it's a good idea for Devon to go with you," Tyler's voice was laced with concern, and I was glad Chance had him for a friend.

That being said, the fact that he wasn't picking up for Tyler worried me.

"I understand," was all I said back.

The phone switched again, and I heard Sadie ask, "Are you okay?"

"I will be. I just want to get Chance and go home. This trip has been...." I paused as I locked eyes with Devon. I stood up and reached for my purse. "Exhausting," I finally settled on.

"Call me on your way back?" she asked. Her question was followed by a quiet giggle and what sounded like Tyler saying something. I had never heard Sadie giggle the entire time we'd been friends.

I shook my head, laughing silently as I told her, "Of course."

I FOUND it comical that Devon and Chance had the same truck. The only difference was that Chance's was black, and Devon's was that creamy vanilla color that looked like frosting.

They also drove the same way: stretched out

with their elbow on the edge of the window, head resting against their hand with their pointer finger sticking up. They were more alike than they realized, and I had a feeling that was also part of their problem.

Both of them were stubborn asses.

"I think it's probably best if I go in by myself. Whatever you wanted to talk to him about can wait until tomorrow," I said as I looked out the window and took in all the new businesses that had popped up in the last twenty-five years.

"As long as you don't skip town first. I may be an ass, but I'd never lay a hand on him. I can't believe the little shit hit me."

I snorted and looked over at him. "Can you blame him? You've done nothing but provoke him at every turn. Newsflash, Devon, YOU'RE the parent, even if you haven't been much of one. He's not the captain of a rival football team. He's your son. Grow up."

He rolled his eyes but didn't say anything as he pulled into a small parking lot that also housed a new —to me—bar that looked packed. The dark building stood on its own, and I could see through the large windows that a small bar was nestled to the right when you walked in. I didn't see Chance sitting there or amidst the people who were crowded around trying to order drinks.

There were no open spots to park, so I told him, "Just drop me off here. I'll make sure we swing by Lynette and George's before we leave tomorrow."

"Are you sure you don't want me to go in with you?"

"You're pushing it as it is. He might have swung on you, but Chance would never do anything to hurt me. His truck is right there. I can drive us back to the hotel." I pointed to Chance's truck, and Devon raised an eyebrow at it and let out a low laugh.

"Alright. I'm sorry, you know. For what happened tonight." He watched me as I got out of the truck, and I turned around to fix him with the most severe stare I could muster.

"There is probably a lot we should discuss if you plan to be part of his life. Because I swear to god, Devon, if you let him down one more time, I will kill you."

He didn't say anything but nodded and motioned for me to get going. So I shut the truck's door and walked around the front to enter the bar. I looked back once more as Devon set about turning around in the cramped lot.

Shaking my head, I went through the door and scanned the room, looking for Chance. It was hard to see with so many people standing around. The music was loud and combined with the din of the bar, it instantly gave me a headache.

Someone in front of me shifted, and I froze as my eyes landed on Chance.

Chance as he kissed Abigail.

My chest tightened as I spun around, a bitter taste rising in my mouth as the sharp sensation of adrenaline surged through me. I felt like the room would cave in, and my breathing became labored as I made my way back out the door.

My body started to tremble as I inhaled vast gulps of air. Tears sprang to my eyes as the tightness in my chest spread, causing my throat to feel like it would close up at any minute.

The sound of a truck picking up speed caused me to look up as Devon drove by, and before I knew what I was doing, I sprinted forward and slapped a hand against the back panel. The brakes sounded as the truck lurched to a stop, and I opened the door and jumped back in.

"Rylee? What the hell? Hey...hey, Rylee, what happened? What's wrong?" Devon's voice sounded far away as I tried to control my breathing.

Tears silently rolled down my cheeks as I attempted to get myself under control. My voice was soft and kept breaking as I asked, "Can you take me back to the hotel, please?"

"Rylee, what the fuck did he say?" Devon put the truck in park, and his hand moved to the door handle like he was about to go cause a scene in the bar.

I shook my head as I bit the inside of my cheek. "Please, Devon. Please just take me back to the hotel."

My head rested against the window as I stared, unseeing, out of it. My mind was painfully recounting every second of the kiss I had witnessed. And every second of the incident from twenty-five years earlier that had been caused by the man sitting next to me.

Tears continued to stream down my face as Devon finally started to drive back in the direction of the hotel, and I whispered in a strangled voice, "The apple doesn't fall far from the tree."

I PACKED IN A HURRY, not surprised to see Devon standing outside the hotel room when I finished. "Why are you still here?"

"Where are you going?" He ignored my question and asked one of his own.

"Home," was my only reply as I started down the hall to the elevator. I had stopped crying while throwing everything I had brought into my bag. An eerie sort of calm had settled over me as if it were blanketing all the pain.

"Are you going to tell me what happened? And how are you going to get home?" he asked as he followed behind me.

I hit the button for the elevator and was glad to find it was still on our floor as the doors opened immediately. "I'll take a Lyft."

"To Jacksonville?" He followed me in, and as the doors shut, he said, "That's ridiculous. I'll take you home."

I didn't argue with him, and for a second—only a split second, my thoughts were of the fact that nothing would piss off Chance more than Devon driving me home.

Devon took my bag from me as we exited and headed to his truck, and I let him without hesitation. He opened my door for me, just like he had when he took me to Butter Rum. But instead of closing the door, he stepped into the open space and asked once more in a gentler tone, "What happened?"

I stared at the dashboard, unwilling to look him in the eyes as that calm blanket peeled back a little. I tempered my emotions and replied, "I learned a hard truth. But it was honestly nothing I didn't already know. Chance belongs with someone his own age, someone like Abigail."

Finally, I turned my head to see a look of remorse on his face. I'd figured he'd had something to do with Abigail being at the party. His guilty stare confirmed it.

"I just want to go home. Please, Devon." My voice was small, and I hated how weak I sounded.

He finally nodded and didn't say anything else as he shut my door, got in the driver's seat, and started the trip to Jacksonville.

My heart was broken, and it was all my fault. It was bad enough that I let my guard down and let Chance in, but I should have let him go as soon as I found out who he was. He would have been fine. I would have been fine–eventually.

Silent sobs racked my body, and I turned away from Devon as I tried to control my tears. The back of my tongue and throat started to hurt from straining to hold them back. I jolted as I felt Devon's hand touch my shoulder, and I shifted as far away from him as I could.

To his credit, he didn't say anything, and he didn't try to touch me again.

AFTER AN HOUR OF SILENCE, I couldn't stand it anymore. So far, I had spent the drive ping-ponging back and forth between extreme heartache and extreme anger. My body was fraught with tension, and at the particular moment I found myself in, I wanted to fight.

I figured I'd never see Devon again after he dropped me off at home, so it didn't matter that I was about to tell him exactly how I felt about him. I was going to throw the biggest fit I'd ever thrown. Everyone else was acting like children today, might as well join them since I certainly couldn't beat them.

"Why'd you do it?"

"Why'd I do what?"

My head spun around, and I glared at Devon, turning my body to face him. I was still wearing my dress from earlier, but I had kicked off my shoes and folded my leg under me so that I could give him my full attention. I wanted to see his face while he answered my questions and listened to what I had to say.

"You know what. Why was I not good enough for you? I gave you *everything*. I trusted you! If you didn't want to be with me, why didn't you just break up with me before you decided to screw someone else?!"

He sighed and looked over at me for a few seconds before turning his attention back to the road. "Do you really want to have this conversation now?"

"Yeah, I want to have it right now. Because once you drop me off, I'm done. I don't ever want to see or hear from you or Chance again." I crossed my arms and looked at him expectantly. It was like we were in high school all over again, having a stupid fight, only this time, it wouldn't end with him sneaking into my room and apologizing with his dick.

Devon made a few attempts to say something before he ran his hand through his hair and shook his head. "I didn't plan it, Rylee. The second I woke up the next morning, I regretted it. I knew, without a doubt, that you were the one I wanted."

"After you fucked someone else?! Devon, we were *friends*. We told each other everything! I would have gladly given you space if you had just told me you wanted to take a break!"

"And how could I expect you to wait around for me while I figured my shit out? Huh, Rylee? You had big plans, but I was never really a part of them. It was always about the life you'd dreamt up for yourself, and I was just along for the ride. What if I had told you I wanted to leave Sandridge? Hell, what if I had told you I wanted to leave Florida? Or that I didn't want to go to Paris? What would you have said then?" he roared back at me.

"ALL OF MY PLANS INCLUDED YOU! How can you even say that? Excuse me for wanting to be successful–for wanting to own a business one day. You were planning on taking over the construction business for George, anyway! You never once mentioned leaving Florida."

"What if I had wanted to travel the world?"

I flailed my hands around and looked at him wide-eyed. "What do you call Paris?!"

He glanced at me, then did a double-take and started to laugh. "You look like a sucker fish."

He'd always compared me to a sucker fish whenever we were fighting, and my mouth would hang open at all the dumb things he'd say. His words were nostalgic, but I closed my mouth and shook my head.

"No, Devon Wiley Eddison, you will not call me a sucker fish and try to lighten the mood. What you did *destroyed* me. That lovesick stupid teenage girl died the day she found out you'd gotten someone else pregnant. And Cherie actually died. It was traumatizing."

Tears sprang to my eyes again, but it was because I was angry, and I wasn't afraid to let these ones fall. "I have spent my entire adult life wondering what is wrong with me, Devon. Wondering what I did to deserve that kind of betrayal. Wondering why I wasn't good enough for you. Any man that has even tried to get close enough, I have pushed away in fear of getting hurt again. I believed there was something truly *wrong* with me that would eventually cause them to leave. All because I made you my world, and you threw it back at me like it never mattered. Like I never mattered!"

"You did matter, Rylee," his voice was soft and quieter this time. "You do matter. You never stopped fucking mattering to me. I made a mistake. And I don't even want to call it that anymore because it gave me Chance, but I never stopped loving you. That's what love is, Rylee. You put your heart out there, and if you're lucky, someone gives theirs back. Only, I'm sorry that I broke yours before you snatched it back and took off in the night. I made choices I'm not proud of either after that. I should have tried harder to get you back. Hell, all these years, and I could have still been trying. But I made peace with what I did and with the fact that I probably would never see you again.

"But something *feral* snapped in me when I saw you at Chance's. One look at you after all these years, and my heart still screamed that you were mine. Or that I was yours anyway. I haven't been given the opportunity to be Chance's father, so it felt more like an enemy was with my girl than it did my son."

After all these years of dreaming about an

apology that I never thought I would get, what I felt as he spoke wasn't closure. It was...nothing. I was overwhelmed by the comment he'd made about Chance, and I found myself switching gears as I told him point blank, "You have been given *every* opportunity to be Chance's father, and you have not taken a single one, Devon."

"Now, that's not fair-"

"What's not fair is that you didn't show up until he was fifteen. Fifteen! That's only three years younger than you were when you conceived him! Can you imagine if George hadn't been in your life until then?"

"I said I'm not proud of my choices when I was younger, Rylee. But I was just a kid. And the life I thought I was gonna have blew up in my face in a matter of weeks."

"So did mine."

He stayed silent, and the GPS on the dash beeped for him to make the turn into my neighborhood. I had less than five minutes to finish saying what I wanted to say, and then I would never see him again.

"Look, Chance never came right out and said it, but I think a part of him wishes that you two had a better relationship. It's not too late, Devon. You might not get to do all the father-son things most dads do, but Chance is a wonderful man. You should try and get to know him."

"That is going to be difficult with you in the

picture, Rylee." It was the truth, and it made me sad, even if I'd already decided to remove myself from the equation.

Devon parked his truck next to my Malibu. At first, I wondered how he knew which car was mine, but then I realized it was the only empty spot. I got out of the truck and went to grab my bag, but he beat me to it and insisted on walking me to my door. I paused a second, wondering if I wanted him to know which unit was mine but then realized it wouldn't be that hard to figure out if he really wanted to, so I started up the stairs to the second floor.

"I'm not in the picture anymore, Devon. You and Chance should try to form some sort of bond."

I unlocked my door and walked in, turning around immediately so that Devon couldn't enter any farther than he already had. He set my bag down and asked me softly, "Are you going to tell me what he did?"

The inside of my cheek was raw from how many times I'd bitten it today, so I bit my lip instead to stop the tears from forming again. Devon's eyes dropped to focus on it, and they darkened. I realized what I'd done and released my lip before I said calmly, "He got me to open up again, and I'll always be grateful for that. But he's also much more like you than he knows, and I won't ruin his life because of a decision he's too young to make."

He stepped closer, and I sucked in a breath. As

much as I cared for Chance, even if I'd decided it was over, I was hurting. And I was only human.

Devon towered over me, his familiar scent of wintergreen and pine filling my senses, and my body tingled as he reached out to cup my cheek. "And us? Do you really never want to see me again?" His voice was strained.

It would be so easy. So easy to give in to him. Easy to let this man, who I had let affect my entire life, sneak back past my defenses and blow my world up once more. My body lit up for him. The simple touch of his hand on my cheek made the room feel too small and too hot.

But my head and heart belonged to the younger version of him I would no longer allow myself to hold on to.

I moved to turn away, but he grabbed my chin and tilted my head up, kissing me without hesitancy. I could have kissed him back and kicked the door shut, sealing all our fates with one easy decision. But one easy decision was what had gotten us into this mess in the first place.

Yanking my head back, I slapped Devon across the face. "Get out."

He blinked and looked confused before he uttered a barely audible, "I'm sorry." Then he left without so much as another word.

My bottom lip trembled as I shut and locked the door behind him. Now that I was alone, I allowed myself to fall apart, sinking into the couch as I dialed Sadie's number.

She picked up on the first ring. "Hey, babe. You back home?"

My sobs were the only thing I could manage to answer her, and she instantly went on alert. "Rylee, what happened? Are you okay?"

"N-no," I managed to stutter. My body shook, and my face scrunched up as everything I had been trying to hold back on the drive poured out.

I curled up in the fetal position as Sadie tried to soothe me. "Hey, hey, now. It's gonna be alright. I'm headed over there, okay?"

"Okay." We hung up, and a picture of Chance and me from our skydiving date stared back at me from my home screen, causing a fresh wave of tears to fall as I turned the phone over and waited for my best friend to arrive.

CHAPTER SIXTEEN

The sunlight filtering through the sheer curtains roused me from sleep, and I instantly regretted not pulling the black-out ones shut before collapsing into bed the night before. I groaned, my head pounding as I lifted myself and reached over to tug one of the thicker curtains closed, casting the room in darkness.

My right hand was sore as fuck, and when I flexed it, the feeling of raw open skin on my knuckles pulled me entirely from sleep.

I collapsed back onto the bed, realizing I still wore my suit from the day before. It was heavy and too warm against my skin. The temperature of the hotel room felt muggy, like the air conditioning never kicked on during the night.

Pulling my phone from my pocket, I realized it was dead and rolled over to plug it in before I headed to the shower. I tried to be quiet, so I wouldn't wake

Rylee, who I assumed was still sleeping in the bed we had shared the first night here.

As I removed my clothes and stepped into the warm spray of the water, flashbacks of the day before filtered through my mind. The party. Asking Rylee if she loved me and not getting the answer I wanted. Our fight.

Devon pulling her into his arms. Her clinging to him.

Rylee's breathy moans as I fucked her angrily.

Me hitting Devon. Fuck, that was why my hand hurt.

I remembered I'd left the party and gone to a local bar, leaving Rylee behind after she had called me a child. And I couldn't blame her because I had acted like one.

I owed my grandparents an apology.

I owed Rylee an apology.

Even though the water felt good against my hand and helped to soothe my headache, I cut my shower short, so I could crawl into bed next to her and tell her how sorry I was.

I dried myself off with a towel and wrapped it around my waist before I brushed my teeth. But as I put my toothbrush back, I realized only my things were spread out on the vanity.

All of Rylee's things were gone.

I went back into the main room as I thought that maybe she'd just packed the night before, ready to go back home as soon as possible today. But when I felt for her on the bed, I realized she wasn't there.

Panic gripped my chest as I clicked on the light and threw open the curtains. All of her stuff was gone. The bed hadn't been slept in. It was like she hadn't even been here.

My phone vibrated on the nightstand, a series of convulses that alerted me to what sounded like a lot of text messages coming through as it sprang back to life. I grabbed it and ran a hand through my damp hair as I saw I had multiple missed calls from Rylee, my grandparents, and Tyler. There was even one from a few hours ago from Abigail.

I opened my texts to read through the ones Rylee had sent.

> Chance, pick up your phone
>
> Babe, I know you're upset. You have every right to be. Will you please just answer my calls?
>
> Chance, where are you?
>
> Are you not coming back to the hotel tonight?

"Fuck," I swore as I hit call.

Her phone rang once before it went to voicemail. So I hung up and tried again, getting the same thing.

I opened the messages from Tyler, and uneasiness wrapped around my very bones as I read them.

Dude, where are you? Rylee said
you left her at your grandparents'
party?

Chance, pick up your phone, man

Chance, what did you do? Shit,
man. You fucked up

Bile rose in my throat, and I ran to the bathroom to relieve my stomach of whatever I had drunk at the bar the night before. I had rarely gotten sick after a night of drinking, except for the one night I'd ever had tequila.

One night, and never again would I touch the stuff. I had blacked out like I'd been roofied and woken up in a pile of my own piss and vomit in Abigail's bed.

But as I threw my guts up into the toilet, the sour taste of it coated my tongue, laced with the unmistakable acidity of lime.

Once I was sure I had nothing more to give to the porcelain bowl in front of me, I brushed my teeth again before I tried to call Rylee once more. Instead of ringing, it went straight to voicemail this time, so I left a message.

"Rylee, I'm so sorry about last night. Where are you? Please call me back."

I hung up and immediately called Tyler, who answered on the first ring, "Chance, what the fuck?"

"I don't know what I did, Ty. All I know is I need

to find Rylee." My voice was strangled and hoarse, and I knew I sounded near panic.

"Chance, she called Sadie as soon as she got home and said you cheated on her. Sadie's been with her all day. She said Rylee refused to get out of bed. Says she's in pretty bad shape."

Cheated on her?

"Tyler, you know I'd never do that." I started racing around the room to throw all my stuff in my bag, so I could get back to Jacksonville as soon as possible, when a knock on the door sounded. Now that I knew Rylee was at her house, I had no clue who it could be.

"She said she saw you, Chance. I'm not doubting you, but...whatever she saw must have been pretty bad."

"Tyler, listen, I have to let you go, but I'll call you as soon as I'm on the road. Tell Sadie I don't know what Rylee saw, but she's got it wrong."

I hung up and redialed Rylee's phone and left another message when her voicemail greeting ended. "Rylee, baby. I don't know what you saw, but you need to let me explain. Please, call me."

There was another knock on the door, and I went over and opened it with excessive force, banging it against the wall.

I was sorely disappointed to find Devon holding two to-go cups of coffee. He looked me over and snorted when he saw I only wore a towel. His eyes roamed over my shoulder, and I tensed as he searched for Rylee.

"Is Abigail here?" he asked.

What the fuck?

My brow raised, and I looked at him suspiciously. "Why the fuck would Abigail be here? What are *you* doing here? How *dare* you show up here and accuse me of cheating on Rylee. Do you want me to hit you again?"

My mind spun from his question. Flashes of dark hair—too dark to be Rylee's—and blue eyes, not hazel—came to me. A girlish giggle as a lime was shoved in my mouth, followed by a kiss.

Fuck. That must have been what Rylee had seen.

I shook my head clear of the images as he scoffed, "I brought Rylee to get you at the bar last night. Your friend Tyler location serviced your ass since you wouldn't answer her calls or messages. But when she went in, she immediately came back out and asked me to bring her here. She was ready to take a Lyft back to Jacksonville, so I offered to drive her. She wouldn't tell me what she saw, only said that, '*the apple didn't fall far from the tree,*' and that, '*you were better off with someone like Abigail.*'"

With every sentence, my heart fractured a bit more, and all the anger I felt left me. Searing pain gripped my chest as I wondered how Rylee must be feeling, what she must have seen. I didn't mean to let it happen. I was angry, and I remembered Abigail showing up and me thinking I should leave.

I recalled Abigail ordering a drink and saying she was there if I needed someone to listen. And I had word vomited everything to her in my bitterness, getting drunker as the night went on.

And she knew, Abigail *knew,* how I got when I drank tequila, which was probably why she had ordered the shots. She'd always had a chip on her shoulder because I broke up with her and left her like our two-year relationship hadn't meant a thing.

I felt like I would be sick again, and I brought my arms up to my head, letting go of the door to go sit on the bed with my head in my hands. I was aware that Devon had come into the room, and my mind turned to thoughts of Rylee in pain and him being there to comfort her.

"Did you guys...?" I couldn't even bring myself to finish that sentence. I couldn't look at him while I waited for his reply, and his silence was deafening.

Finally, he replied, "No, son. We didn't. But I'll be honest, it wasn't from my lack of trying. I drove her home–to her condo, not your house."

Bile rose in my throat again.

"I took her bag upstairs for her."

I breathed deep in through my nose and out through my mouth while shoving my palms into my eyes.

"And I kissed her."

My heart felt like it had dropped into my stomach.

"Then she slapped me and told me to get out."

Did that make me feel a little better? I couldn't tell.

"We both fucked up yesterday, Chance." He stood from where he was seated on the small loveseat in the sitting room and walked over to sit on the other bed across from me as he handed me the other coffee.

"Drink this. It will help with the headache I'll bet you're feeling right now."

It was the most fatherly thing he'd ever done for me, and I could tell he knew that's what I was thinking by the look he gave me when I took it.

"It's my fault Abigail was at the party yesterday. I remembered hearing about her from your grandma. So I did some digging and sought her out. I told her you'd be thrilled to see her and that I would be happy to help her get you back."

I stood up and moved to grab some clothes, not wanting to continue this conversation in a towel. Devon seemed to understand and didn't say anything as I changed in the bathroom and emerged a minute later. I sat back on the bed and took a long drink of the bitter black liquid he'd given me.

"I don't get it," I eventually said. "I understand that you hate me. I get that I ruined your life. But why can't you just move on? Why do you keep *trying* to hurt me?"

I braced myself for him to validate what I had said. With Rylee between us, I knew it was just one more thing to make him dislike me. And it was one more thing to add to the list of reasons I felt why I was better off without him in my life.

"First off, I don't hate you. I know I've made a lot of bad mistakes in my lifetime, but you are not one of them, Chance. Claire and Collin did a better job raising you than I could have ever hoped to. And I'm sorry that I've never been there. By the time I thought I was ready to have a relationship with you, you wanted nothing to do with me, so I acted out in anger instead of understanding where you were coming from.

"I honestly thought you were better off without me, Chance. That's why I stopped trying to see you. But when your grandparents mentioned they wanted you at their party, I don't know. I thought that maybe we could try and start over."

He paused in his story, and I watched as he looked like he was struggling with what he wanted to say next. "But then I saw Rylee," he started after he swallowed thickly. "I hadn't seen her since we were kids. One day, I came home after football practice to a moving truck in her driveway. Her parents wouldn't let me see her. Her overdramatic little sister screamed at me and kept asking me why I did it. But I didn't have an answer for her then.

"The truth was, I was scared. Rylee had big dreams, and I was afraid I wouldn't live up to them. She wanted to leave after high school and travel to France. She wanted to open her own bakery in Sandridge and planned to make it so popular she could open a few more in neighboring towns. She had a busy life plotted. Every t was crossed, and every i dotted. She even planned our hypothetical kids. Their names, the years she wanted to be pregnant, and what months she wanted the birthdays.

"It was a lot of responsibility. And even though it was a life I had agreed to, I didn't know if I wanted it. I only knew I wanted *her*. And I grew scared that I would fuck it up somehow. Then I did, the night I spent with your mother."

Hearing him talk about Rylee in that manner was strange. It didn't sound at all like the Rylee that I knew. She hated making plans unless it was planning cake flavors for the bakery. And I wondered if it was just another thing she changed about herself after Devon hurt her.

But hearing him bring up my birth mother was like a punch to the gut. I had only ever heard anything about her from Claire and had never spent time with anyone else who had known her besides Rylee. Even Devon's parents didn't know much about her. I could tell it was a sore subject for Rylee, but she'd still told me what she knew, which didn't go beyond '*she had a difficult life at home*' and '*she was quiet.*'

"Your mom was kind. She was quiet, and I'm sure Claire told you they had a rough life at home with Cherie's father. But despite having a crappy life at home, she always had a smile for anyone willing to look at her. She was an extremely talented artist.

And I think she would have had an excellent sense of adventure if she had been given the opportunity.

"The night we conceived you, we randomly struck up a conversation on the beach. She was sketching her view of the ocean, and I commented on how good I thought it was. I offered her a drink while we talked, and before I knew it, I was waking up the next morning with her tucked into my side. She promised she wouldn't say anything, and I took her home before finding out that people had seen us and had already told Rylee."

He was silent for a few minutes, and I dared not say a word to interrupt or even ask a question. This was the most anyone had ever told me about my parents' lives. And I didn't realize how starved I'd been for their story until now.

"You don't know what you have until it's gone, Chance. The second I knew I had lost her, I knew I wanted every single one of her plans. And for a little while, I thought that she might forgive me. We were friends for so long before we dated that if anything, we could still be at least that, even if it killed me. It would have been better than losing her completely."

He paused again, and I heard myself fill in the next part. "But then my mother found out she was pregnant."

Devon nodded. "And everything I'd been so scared of had come true. In one night, with one conversation, I changed my whole life. And I'll be honest, for a long time, I did blame you, Chance. But

I was coming to try and make amends. Or at least try and open a line of communication that didn't result in hostility between us.

"And when it was Rylee on the other side of your door, I thought fate had decided to grant me a second chance. Until I saw you and realized the situation, and then I just went into defense mode. There were honestly a few seconds where I wondered if she knew who you were and was out for revenge. I was torn between wanting to protect you and internally freaking out because I hadn't seen her in so long.

"But by how she acted, I quickly realized she didn't know. And then my anger turned to you—the man who was now playing house with the only woman I've ever loved. I childishly clocked you as a competitor. Watching you two together was one of the most painful things I've ever experienced. But I am sorry for the way that I acted."

I gave a slight shrug as I looked down at my coffee cup. "I'm sorry we made a scene at grandma and grandpa's party, but I'm not sorry I hit you."

He laughed, and it caused me to crack a smile too. This was the most we'd ever talked. And even though my insides were twisting with every passing minute I couldn't speak to Rylee, part of me was glad to be having this conversation because part of me *had* always wanted a better relationship with my father.

"I spent my whole life thinking that you just absolutely hated me. Once I became a teenager, I realized I didn't really care to know you anymore.

But part of me always wondered if we would ever be able to have a real father-son relationship. But I don't know how to do that moving forward, Devon. I don't know how to be around you and Rylee, and always wonder if you two are thinking about each other. Or wonder if we'll wake up one day, and she'll realize she'd rather be with you."

His deep laugh reverberated throughout the room, and a hint of annoyance flashed through me. "I don't understand what's so funny."

"I won't lie to you, Chance. Rylee has always been it for me. Sure, there have been other women throughout the years, but I always compared them to her. Even in my adult life, even though I never got to know her past seventeen. So, I can't promise you that I won't watch her at family get-togethers and wonder what life would have been like. But Rylee made it very clear there was never any competition. If it came down to you or me, she'd always choose you, son."

DEVON STUCK AROUND for a little longer, waiting patiently while I continuously paused the rest of our conversation to try and get ahold of Rylee. She still wouldn't answer, and I wondered if she'd turned off her phone when every call started going straight to voicemail.

"Give her some time, Chance. She's pretty upset.

I think it reminded her of what she went through with me," Devon said as he stood to leave.

I'd told him what had happened and what Abigail had done. I'd also texted Abigail and told her never to contact me again, and then I blocked her number.

"That's why I don't want to give her any time. I don't need her to spend it thinking the worst. I just want to move forward with our lives already," I explained as I walked him to the door.

"Well, for your sake and hers, I hope she's willing to hear you out." He started walking down the hall in the direction of the elevator.

I called out to him, "Hey, Devon?"

He turned and looked at me expectantly. And I felt a little of the weight lifted off my shoulders as I smiled at him. "Thank you."

He smiled back, a genuine smile, not a smug grin or a smirk. "You're welcome, son."

CHAPTER SEVENTEEN

I WAS SURE I HAD EXPELLED ALL THE TEQUILA I drank the night before already, but my stomach was still unsettled the entire drive home. The thought of Rylee walking into the bar last night and seeing the one split-second that Abigail had kissed me had me completely distraught.

If the roles had been reversed, and I had gone through what she did with Devon, and then I had walked in on what looked like her kissing another man, it would be enough to break my heart and build a wall around it so high no one would ever be able to breach it again.

Her phone was turned off, and I was only about ten minutes away from town when Sadie's number popped up on my screen. Relief coursed through my body as I hit accept. "Sadie, how is she?"

I heard the tall blonde sigh on the other end of the phone, and she sounded exhausted as she said,

"Not good, Chance. How would you be if you'd seen her making out with your dad after what happened yesterday?"

"I swear it wasn't like that, Sadie. She just happened to see the exact moment my ex kissed me, but I pushed her away, I swear. I'm almost back. I'm going straight to her house so I can explain."

"I just left there. I don't think it's a good idea for you to go there right now, Chance. She's already had a bottle of wine to herself and won't eat. She knows you're trying to reach her, but she doesn't want to talk. You didn't even try to call her until this morning. She is assuming the worst, and I don't think there's going to be anything you can say to change her mind right now."

A flash of irritation seared my chest. "So I'm just supposed to go home and wait for her to come to me? Come on, Sadie. We both know that's not the right move here. She needs to hear from me how sorry I am and that what she saw isn't what she thinks it is."

"I don't think she needs to see you right now, Chance. I'm telling you, as her best friend, I don't think it's a good idea for you to go over there."

As I entered the city, I headed toward Rylee's house instead of my own. I was done with the space and the time, and I didn't care what Sadie said. Rylee and I were going to get through this and move on from this situation. No more misunderstandings.

"I'll talk to you later, Sadie. I'm about to get to her place."

She sighed, "Don't say I didn't warn you, pup."

I pulled into Rylee's apartment complex, the anxiety and anger that flowed through me caused my stomach to clench in knots. All I wanted was to crawl into bed with Rylee in my arms and sleep for a day. I was exhausted, and I missed my girl. I hated fighting with her. And a small part of me wondered if this is how it would always be.

Especially if I wanted to attempt any sort of relationship with Devon.

I took the stairs two at a time and almost let myself in before realizing I should knock instead. The heat was sweltering today, and sweat dripped down my back as I waited for her to answer the door. It took me moving from a polite two knocks at once to nearly pounding on the door as I shouted, "Rylee, I know you're in there. Let me in!" for her to finally come to the door.

I'd assumed she'd have red eyes and a puffy nose, hair thrown up on the top of her head, and in pajamas. But instead, she looked freshly showered and put together like any other day. She wore a pair of black linen shorts with a white shirt that fell off one shoulder. Her hair had been left to dry in its natural waves, and she was even wearing makeup. Her signature pink lips turned down in a frown when she saw it was me making a scene outside her condo.

"What are you doing here?" she sounded calm and collected, and it threw me off. I didn't know what to expect, but this wasn't it.

"Rylee, I'm so sorry. What you saw last night wasn't what you thought it was. You saw the worst part you could have seen. I pushed her away, I swear." I moved forward to pull her into my arms, but she stepped back out of my reach and crossed her arms over her stomach.

"Yeah. I got your messages. There was a reason I didn't respond to them." Her brow furrowed, and I looked at her expectantly, waiting for her to say something else.

When she didn't, I took a few steps inside and closed the door behind me. I turned around again to find that all the moving boxes we had packed up already had been cut open and her stuff returned to various spots around the living room.

"Rylee, I know you're upset. You have every right to be. Devon came by this morning and told me everything. He's the one who asked Abigail to come to the party." It wasn't the most mature thing to do, but I hoped that perhaps her anger toward him would trump what she was feeling toward me, and we could shift our focus to the beginning of our problematic trip.

"I know," was all she said.

"Can you just talk to me? Please?" I pleaded. I tried to take a step closer to her, but as soon as I advanced, she retreated the same distance.

"I don't want to talk right now, Chance. Honestly, there's not much to say. I think it would be best if we went our separate ways."

"I know you're upset, baby. And you have every right to be. But I'm not going to just let you walk away from me. And frankly, I'm tired of playing this game with you. You said you were all in. So you can't just turn and tuck tail whenever something hard happens."

The words were meant to spark some sort of emotion from her, but she stared at me with blank eyes. No hurt was shining in them, no unshed tears, and her posture was relaxed. Meanwhile, nausea started to creep along the lining of my stomach caused by uneasiness due to her calm disposition.

"Come on, Rylee. We're not doing this anymore. Talk to-"

"Devon kissed me," she interrupted.

Before I could tell her that I knew and that it didn't matter because I also knew that she'd slapped him and told him to leave, she kept going.

"It would have been easy, you know. To keep letting him kiss me. Let him stay and comfort me the way I thought Abigail comforted you last night. But I didn't because it would have been petty. It would have been what someone your age would have done. It's what you did. You left me at a party to go get drunk with your ex. Whether you meant for it to happen or not, it did. And I realize you were upset, but I also realize that it isn't fair of me to ask you to handle things the way someone my age would."

"Can you just stop being condescending for a minute, Rylee? Plenty of men your age still play games, and they still fuck up. Yes, Abigail kissed me. But SHE kissed ME. I'm sorry that you walked out before you saw me push her away-"

"And what happened after that, Chance? Because Devon took me back to the hotel to pack, and then we left. During all of that, there would have been enough time for you to catch us before we'd gone. But you didn't even call me until this morning. So whether you spent the night with Abigail or by yourself, you didn't even think of me until this morning." Her voice was still deadly calm, and it was starting to scare me. She spoke in a monotone manner and still didn't even look upset.

Tyler had once told me something I hadn't paid attention to before. He'd said that when your partner is still yelling, crying, and arguing with you, it means they still care. That they are still willing to fight for the relationship.

But, when no tears come, and all the fight has drained out of the conversation, it's as good as over to them. They've already decided to harden their heart to you, and good luck getting them to change their mind.

And the truth was she was right. I pushed Abigail away, but I didn't leave. I sat alone at the bar until it closed, before I returned to the hotel. I'd felt guilty, but I had been too mad to go back and face Rylee. Once I'd made it back to the hotel, I'd purposefully collapsed into the bed I knew she wouldn't be in. Partly to not disturb her but also because I hadn't been ready to talk to her.

Rylee gave me a tiny smile and a slight shrug. "We tried, Chance. But I think it's best if we cut our losses. It's too much drama. And I think that you and Devon should talk. It would be good for you both. I told him the same thing. You're more alike than you realize. Like father, like son."

Her words hit me like a physical blow. The air rushed out of me, and my chest was crushed with an intense pressure that made me feel like I couldn't breathe. My voice broke as I shook my head and insisted, "Rylee, you don't mean that."

I swear her face faltered for a second before she straightened and nodded. "I do, Chance. This is exactly why I said I don't do relationships. It hurts to end them."

"Yeah, you look pretty okay to me," I snapped. Growing up, Claire had always told me it was perfectly normal and acceptable for a man to cry. That it didn't make a man any less to show his emotions. But as I stared at Rylee, I clenched my teeth so hard to keep myself from shedding tears that I thought they might crack.

Her face softened as she said gently, "You'll move on, Chance. You'll be just fine. I'm not the great love of your life that you're losing. Just a lesson along the way to find her."

I bit out a sharp laugh. "Thanks for deciding that for me."

She didn't say anything else but looked at the floor as I felt the tears start to line my eyes. I'd had enough and turned to leave. With my hand on the doorknob, I paused and whispered, my voice barely audible as it cracked, "Goodbye, Rylee."

I left without another look back. But I stayed on the other side of her door once it shut behind me. I heard the click of the lock and the sound of her releasing a stuttered breath as the tears I'd expected her to have, finally fell, and her sobs could be heard through the barrier between us.

Every fiber in my body screamed at me to turn around and demand she let me back in so I could hold her, and it took everything I had to force my feet to move. The sounds of her cries faded the closer I got to my truck.

While the sound of her breaking down crushed my heart, it also pained me to admit that it sparked an ember of hope.

CHAPTER EIGHTEEN

Chance

A LITTLE OVER A WEEK PASSED, AND I DIDN'T hear from Rylee. Devon had reached out a few times, but I wasn't in the mood to talk to him. Part of me wondered if they were talking, but a bigger part knew she wouldn't do that to me. And I honestly didn't think Devon would anymore, either.

A random Tuesday found me in a pair of board-shorts lounging on my back patio, drunk on a bottle of Glen, but I couldn't tell you which Glen had shown up to my pity party. Domino perched at the edge of my lounge chair, his tail flicking back and forth as he stared at me with displeasure in his green eyes.

"Don't look at me like that," I muttered as I flicked my sunglasses up and fixed him with a glare of my own.

Gary, who was lounging in the pool again, let out a throaty grumble, and my gaze lazily turned to him as I let my glasses slip back over my eyes. "Don't you start, too, bud. Or these little pool time playdates will come to an end."

He groaned again and agitatedly kicked a foot like a kid throwing a tantrum.

"Are you talking to your pets again? Dude, you gotta leave the house," Tyler's voice sounded from my left.

"They're judging me because their mom abandoned them." I shrugged and took another sip of my drink.

"I think they're judging you because you smell like a distillery." Tyler sat in the chair next to mine and picked up the scotch. Glenlivet stared at me from the label as he tossed back a swig straight from the bottle.

I grimaced. "I don't know where your mouth has been, dude. Get a glass."

He grinned over at me and waggled his eyebrows. "I can tell you where it's gonna be. I'm this close to getting Sadie to crack. Her husband was photographed with another leggy model yesterday. A redhead this time. Sadie hates gingersnaps. I give it another week before she finally admits there's something between us. Then my mouth is going to be all up and down that insane fucking body, between those luscious legs-"

"Cut it out, man, it's too early for that shit," I complained as I sunk further into my chair.

"It's four in the afternoon, Chance. You should

212

get cleaned up. You've gotta do the hedges at Sugar and Scotch today," Tyler said nonchalantly as he reached over and scratched Domino on the head.

Domino's ears flattened, and a second later, he swiped at Tyler's hand with a hiss. I felt like doing the same, but I figured it might be a little weird coming from me.

"Get one of the guys to do it." I had been neglecting work, and Tyler had picked up the slack without so much as a peep. But I'd be damned if my first job in over a week was going to be there.

"They're closing up early tonight cause it's slow. Sadie told me to tell you no one would be there after eight. They like the way you do it."

It was a shit excuse, and Tyler knew it. But that tiny spark of hope flared to life in my chest at his words. To me, it sounded like he and Sadie were scheming. And if they were scheming, then it meant Rylee must be as miserable as I currently was.

"No one is gonna be there?" I turned my head slightly enough so that he wouldn't be able to tell if I were looking at him, but I could still gauge his reaction.

"Not to my knowledge." Tyler started examining his nails, a very non-Tyler trait. Did he even realize we'd been friends for nearly seven years?

I stretched out, causing Domino to jump down and pad to the pool's edge, where Gary looked like he was gearing up to get out. "Let my water puppy out in the backyard once he's ready, will you?"

Tyler scrunched his nose and shook his head vigorously. "Nope. That's a hard pass. Will not do, sir. As a matter of fact, I'll be going now."

Gary let out a loud grunt, and I swore Tyler picked up his pace as he headed back through the sliding glass doors that led to the kitchen. "Don't forget the hedges!" he yelled over his shoulder before disappearing around the corner.

TYLER HAD SAID Sugar and Scotch would be closed by eight, so I made sure not to arrive until eight-thirty. I'd showered and sobered up, and once the Glenlivet was–mostly–out of my system, I'd begun to rethink my decision to go.

The hedges looked like shit, and I was annoyed that Tyler hadn't been keeping up with them. But whether or not that was part of his and Sadie's plan– and I knew they had a plan–was to be determined. I pulled my truck around back, and adrenaline rushed through me as I saw Rylee's red Malibu parked in its usual spot.

As I parked my truck, small droplets of rain started to fall from the sky. A typical light summer sprinkle that would pass soon, but while I waited, I noticed that the damn back door was ajar, propped open with a brick.

Damnit, Rylee.

The rain passed quickly, and I got out of my

truck to grab what I needed out of the back, purposefully loud, knowing that the noise would carry into the kitchen. The scent of cinnamon wafted out, a nostalgic telltale sign that she was in the middle of or had just finished baking something.

I missed that smell in my house. I missed coming home to her baking in my kitchen. I fucking missed *her*.

Her voice cut distantly through the quiet of the night, a soft curse followed by hurried steps down the short hallway that led to the backdoor. I was sure she'd heard me and was coming to make sure no one was trying to break into her car. I turned my back to the door and started cutting away at the overgrown foliage.

The rain started again, this time more than a drizzle. Within seconds my white shirt was plastered to my body, and the air was filled with the light scent of wet grass as the aroma of cinnamon was washed away.

I heard the door slam open all the way and turned at the noise, knowing I'd see Rylee there. But even if I'd known it, the image of her standing in the rain still took my breath away. She was holding what looked like a small canister of what I assumed was pepper spray, arms raised like she was about to set it off. But when she saw me, her arms fell helplessly to her sides, and I could visibly see her let out a sigh of relief.

"I thought you were trying to break into my car,"

was all she said, her voice muffled slightly by the sound of the rain falling around us.

I turned and kept working on the hedge in front of me. "I see you're still leaving the back door open."

"What are you doing here, Chance?" she asked as if it weren't obvious.

I kept my voice level as I responded, "Working. What's it look like?"

"Tyler said he'd be sending one of the other guys tomorrow."

So he and Sadie *had been* scheming. Those brilliant bastards.

It didn't escape me how her eyes roamed my body when I turned around to face her. "Well, I'm the one doing it. And I was told no one would be here. So, if you'll excuse me, I have a job to finish."

She huffed as I turned back around, and moments later, I felt her hand on my arm as she attempted to turn me back around. I barely budged but humored her and turned to look at her over my shoulder again. "What, Rylee?"

"Are you really going to act like that, Chance? You're gonna treat me like shit because of what happened?" Her brows were furrowed together, and her hands were held out at her sides. She looked fucking sexy, soaking wet in her cut-off jean shorts and the same navy top she'd been wearing our first night together.

The rain started coming down in a sheet, making it near impossible to keep our eyes open. "Go inside,

Rylee. I'll come back some other time to finish the job."

I turned, and it caused her to take a step back so our chests weren't pressed against each other. The look in her eye was familiar as she searched my face, her chest heaving with labored breaths. She wanted me, and it made my heart soar to know I still had that effect on her. I took a step toward her, and she took a step back.

"Go inside, Rylee," I repeated, lowering my voice to a tone I knew made her wet and not from the rain.

She swallowed thickly as the rain let up once more. "I know what you're doing."

"So why are you still standing here?" I took another step, and she held her ground. I raised an eyebrow at the resolve on her face and took one more so that our chests nearly touched.

She didn't say anything as I reached up and gently ran the back of my fingers against her cheek. Her eyes fluttered closed as her head shifted ever so slightly into my touch. "Chance...."

"Don't make it complicated," I whispered. "Just do whatever feels right."

My words caused her to open her eyes, a fierce determination shining in her hazel orbs. *There you are, baby.*

She surged forward with enough force that it knocked me back a step as she launched into my arms and crushed her lips to mine. Her hands fisted in my shirt, pulling me with her as she backed up toward the building. The door was still wide open, and as we crossed the threshold, I finally pulled back, only long enough to pull the door shut and lock it behind me.

We both dripped water down the hall as she continued to pull me to the kitchen. Once we got into the open room, the scent of cinnamon hit me full force as Rylee peeled my shirt over my head. She took her shirt off next as my hands quickly worked the button on her shorts and shoved them down her legs.

She was wearing a sky blue lace bra and under-wear set, her breasts heaving behind the wet see-through material, her rose-colored nipples pebbled so I could see their outline through the fabric. I leaned down and closed my mouth around one, nipping at it as she arched her back and pushed her chest into me.

I grabbed her by her hips and lifted her onto the large stainless steel prepping table in the middle of the room, peeling her underwear down before I removed my jeans. She was panting and making little mewling noises like she couldn't wait for me to be inside her, and my cock stood at attention, ready to find its home inside her warm pussy.

"Fuck, I missed this. I missed you," I said before I pulled down the cup of her bra and sucked her other nipple into my mouth. My fingers moved between her legs that she held open, just waiting for me to fill the space between them.

"Chance, please," she begged, and it was the sweetest sound I'd ever heard.

"Please, what? Use your words, Rylee," I commanded as I ran my fingers up her wet center to her clit. She bucked her hips against my hand and reached down to grip my cock as she stroked me, twisting her hand just the way I liked.

"Fuck me, Chance. I need you to fuck me," she whined before she pulled my head closer to kiss me again.

I indulged her kiss for mere seconds, sweeping my tongue against hers before I pulled back, removing her hand as I grabbed her ankles and pulled her legs wide. I leaned down to circle my tongue around her clit, her hands finding my head as she pushed me closer. Her breathy moans were like music to my ears as I sucked and nibbled on her.

My eyes traveled up her body as I feasted on her, watching as she writhed against my tongue. Back bowed and head tilted back, her eyes screwed shut as she gripped my hair and started to ride my face. My lips pillowed around her clit, continuously sucking it into my mouth, the suction noises joining her cries of pleasure as she neared her release.

The grip she had on my hair bordered almost as painful as my throbbing cock. Her breathing grew labored as her orgasm crested, and when she came on my tongue, I didn't drink her down but instead stood and pulled her to the edge of the table before I thrust into her. She repeatedly cried out my name, still riding her first release as her walls fluttered around my dick.

"You look so beautiful when you come for me, baby," I said as I reached down to draw an arm around her shoulders so I could pull her up to a sitting position. We were nearly eye to eye as I dropped my hand to grip her hip. The new angle allowed me to hit that spot deep inside her, making her eyes roll back in her head, and I picked up my pace.

"Let me see you. Look at me, Rylee," I demanded. She obeyed, and I gripped her chin with my other hand to watch while she came undone and climaxed again. The intimacy caused my release to pour through me, and I kept moving inside her, feeling as she clenched those inner walls around me with each thrust. And before I could stop myself, I opened my mouth and said, "I love you."

I regretted it the second the words left me, knowing it was the wrong time to say it as her expression changed. She froze, and the tension in the air immediately shifted from sex-charged to awkward. I stopped moving and pulled back, and she let me, hopping down from the table to find her clothes. We didn't say anything as we dressed, and a sick feeling of disappointment ran through me when she turned to me with regret in her eyes.

"This was a mistake," her words were barely audible, but at least this time, she wasn't an emotionless statue.

I knew she still cared for me, and I called her out on it. "Stop lying to yourself, Rylee. Just admit that you love me. You know that you do. I know that you do. Even Sadie and Tyler know it. I know that I hurt you, but you're hurting me, too. Does that count for nothing?" I tried to move closer to her, but she held out a hand, silently telling me to stop.

"I'm sorry, Chance. I don't love you," she lied. We both knew it wasn't the truth. But it didn't hurt any less to hear her say the words out loud. My sinuses burned as I backed away, and good ol' Glen felt like he might pop back up from my stomach. I couldn't keep doing this to myself. It was hurting her. It was hurting me.

And I didn't want either of us to hurt anymore.

My voice was hoarse and cracked as I said, "You know, I'm not my dad, Rylee. You're making a mistake, and you know it. You're running again because you're scared, and I get it because I'm scared too. But I can't keep doing this back and forth. I'm not going to chase you anymore. You win, I'm done. Goodbye, Rylee."

As I walked down the hall, my heart shattered, and I didn't wait to see if she'd break down this time. I was already spiraling. I needed to let her go, or I'd end up just like Devon had.

Like father like son, indeed.

CHAPTER NINETEEN

Rylee

The back door to Sugar and Scotch was unlocked and propped open when I got there the evening after I'd made the mistake of sleeping with Chance in the kitchen. I had promised myself I wouldn't go there with him again, no matter how good he looked or how much I missed him.

But fuck he *had* looked so good in the rain. And I was weak when it came to him. It had been so hard to stay away, to continue to convince myself that it would be best for everyone involved. That it would be better for him and Devon to have a relationship if I weren't in the picture.

I was lying to myself, though. I wanted him. God, did I want him. And he wanted me, too. But it wasn't an easy decision when it continued to hurt other people and continued to hurt ourselves. We had been doing a great job of staying away from each other, and I had a feeling the night before had only happened because Sadie and Tyler had decided they'd both had enough of our moping.

Sadie's HOT Couture by Givenchy perfume floated down from the kitchen, and I could hear hushed whispers as I moved closer, careful not to make a sound so I could listen to what else those two morons were planning.

"It can be our little secret," Tyler's quiet voice reached my ears.

I huffed inwardly. Of course, they were planning something else.

"Tyler, I can't," Sadie's voice sounded strained.

I shifted closer, trying to peek around the corner without alerting them to my presence.

"Stop lying to yourself, Sadie. Your marriage is over. You know it, I know it, your husband knows it. The whole of fucking New York knows it. Stop trying to be a saint when we both know all you want to do right now is get on your knees and commit a sin."

Wait, what the hell did I just walk into?

I knew it would only be a matter of time before Sadie fell for Tyler. Her husband treated her like absolute shit and publicly stepped out on her all the time. I had often encouraged her to have a little fun with Tyler over the last few months. But the kitchen had already been christened, and I felt bad enough as it was about having sex in a place where I baked the food that we sold. I hadn't left last night for another two hours as I scrubbed every surface of this place. Even the ones we hadn't touched.

I rounded the corner, and my eyes grew wide as Tyler's lips had just barely met Sadie's before she jumped back due to my presence. I'd just interrupted their first kiss.

Fuck my life.

"I am so sorry, guys."

Tyler's hand was suspended in the air from where he had been holding onto Sadie's neck before he dropped it as she rushed out to the bar without a word. He sighed before turning to look at me with the most severe look I'd ever seen him give anyone.

"Chance told me what happened last night," he stated, like I hadn't just caught them kissing.

"Yeah, thanks for that. I wondered why Sadie insisted on me making the cinnamon rolls last night. I should have known you two were up to something." I headed out to the bar to talk to my friend about what had just happened, but she was occupied with customers down at the end. Tyler followed close behind me, rounding the bar to take a seat on a stool.

I poured us both a shot of Jameson, and we knocked them back, neither of us saying anything afterward. I filled our glasses again, but instead of shooting his, he took a sip before placing it back on the bar.

"He loves you, you know. Like, truly, madly, deeply, loves you. You're it for him. He won't recover if you say goodbye for real," Tyler said softly, playing with the edge of a napkin in the stack next to him.

His eyes kept skirting over to Sadie, who was keeping herself busy away from us.

"Sometimes love isn't enough, Tyler. This whole situation is so fucked up. I've been letting the whole thing with Devon affect my whole life, and it's just time to let it all go. Chance deserves to have a relationship with his father. They can't do that with me in the picture."

"So let it all go then. Devon has nothing to do with you and Chance, Ry. Chance is an adult. And he'll do anything you need him to, to make things right. That's what you do when you love someone. You're willing to risk it all. Even your heart, knowing there's a possibility the person you're giving it to will tear it to shreds."

His words reminded me of what Devon had said to me on our drive back to Jacksonville, and I followed his gaze back to my best friend as my eyes softened. "Is that what you're doing?"

His eyes found mine quickly. "I'd do anything for her, and she knows it. If she needs a friend, I'll be there. A shoulder to cry on? I'll be the tissue. She wants me to fuck her six ways from Sunday, I'll give her the best damn time of her life and won't ask for anything in return. Hell, I'd go up to the city and off her husband if that's what she wanted. All she's gotta do is ask. But she's gotta *ask* me. She's gotta stop being so damn afraid of her feelings. So do you.

226

"Make up your mind." He hopped off the stool and headed toward the door. "Don't make him wait forever, though. And if you're really done, don't keep leading him on with late nights in the kitchen."

I had a feeling his parting sentence was louder so that maybe he could give Sadie that same warning.

"ARE we going to talk about it?" I asked as I side-eyed Sadie while we cleaned up behind the bar after we'd closed.

"Nope. We gonna talk about *your* late-night rendezvous?" she asked as she wiped down the tops of the bottles in the well.

I shook my head. "Nope."

We were both silent as we worked around each other. At least ten minutes passed before we turned to each other at the same time and simultaneously exclaimed loudly, "Okay, I need to talk about it!"

Laughter bubbled up between us as we took a seat at the bar and launched into the woes of the younger men that had started to consume our lives.

"So, how was your first kiss with Tyler?" I prodded as I nudged Sadie's shoulder with mine.

She shrugged and tilted her head down so that her hair fell over her face, hiding it from view. "It was barely a kiss before you walked in. But I swear he is the most persistent pup, so eager to please. I know Scott has his dalliances, but I never wanted to have that kind of marriage. But if Tyler keeps it up, he *will* be my dirty little secret. And speaking of dirty secrets, did you really think Chance wouldn't tell Tyler what you two did? He called him when he got home. He sounded pretty shaken up."

"Oh, so you were with Tyler last night, too? Do you two just hang out every night now? Are you sure you're not low-key dating?" I joked.

Sadie didn't laugh as she fixed me with a stare, and I knew she was about to hit me with some hard truths that I wasn't sure I was ready to hear. I sighed and readied myself for whatever it was she was about to say.

"What are you doing, Ry? You're doing the same thing you did twenty-five years ago, babe. Chance makes you happy. You love him. I know you do. So why are you making excuses not to be with him?" She shifted in her seat so that she could look at me while she spoke, and I felt exposed under her gaze. My chest felt like it had been flayed open, and I felt vulnerable.

My words sounded like a broken record, even to my ears, as I replied, "He needs to have a relationship with Devon. He needs-"

"Oh, cut the bullshit, Rylee. Why are you letting Devon get between you? They can do their daddy-son shit on their own time. They are grown-ass adults. If Devon isn't over you, it's his own damn fault. It's been twenty-five years. You both need to get the fuck over it. Time to move this train along,

Rylee. Chance sounded like he'd had it last night. You will never forgive yourself if you lose him for good. And you can't expect him to sit around and wait for you, even if he does love you. He's gotta have some respect for himself. And hearing the love of your life say she doesn't love you? Well, I'm assuming that was a hard pill for him to swallow. Even if he knew you were lying through your teeth."

"Geeze, Sadie. Tell me how you really feel," I deadpanned.

"I can keep going if you'd like," she lilted with a smile.

"I'd like it if you took your own advice. That's what I'd like."

"Yeah, well. Easier said than done, as the saying goes, I suppose." She got off her stool to finish cleaning behind the bar as I contemplated my choices.

Easier said than done. Exactly. I'd pushed Chance away, and for what? For him and Devon to maybe take a few fishing trips and have dinner at George and Lynette's? I was still letting Devon dictate my life all these years later. Or perhaps I was just scared to let it go because I'd built my entire life around what he'd done.

But maybe it was time to start celebrating it. After all, it had given us Chance. And I was a fool to continue trying to convince myself that I wasn't in love with him. Even he'd known it when I lied to him the night before. We'd hurt each other, but we were in love. I need to run toward that, not away from it.

Nothing in life was guaranteed. Maybe we'd break up in another few months. Maybe it wouldn't work out.

But it could. And maybe we'd make it to that beach wedding Chance had dreamed up for us the first night we'd hung out.

I only hoped my crippling fear of ruining his life hadn't destroyed our opportunity to be happy together.

"Sadie? Do you still have Big Al's number?"

"The bartender from Pascal's? Yeah, why?" She looked at me with an odd look as she took the glasses out of the dishwasher.

"I have an idea."

And I hoped I wasn't too late.

CHAPTER TWENTY

LEAVING RYLEE TUESDAY NIGHT HAD LEFT ME
an empty shell of the man I'd been before her.

I never knew your heart could hurt so badly
without literally stopping. But that's what it felt like.
There was a hole the size of her fist in my chest
where she'd pulled it out and crushed it.

When I first met Tyler, he'd been coming out of
a bad breakup. I remembered thinking that ending a
relationship couldn't possibly hurt as much as he'd
described. And I had been right.

It was worse.

So, here I was at Saturday night karaoke, waiting
for a random girl who had given me her number at
the grocery store of all places after asking me to reach
something off the top shelf for her.

Tyler's words echoed in my head from earlier
that morning when I told him what I was doing.
"Normally, I would say go for it, but I don't think

you're ready, and I don't think the term 'the way to get over someone is to get under another' applies here."

It figured he would still be rooting for Team Rylee. After all, he and Sadie had grown close these last few months, and I was sure he didn't want to lose his connection with her. But I had no intention of doing anything with the bottle-blonde that wore too much makeup other than having a drink. I wasn't ready. But I was tired of moping around the house, and I had a feeling I was starting to annoy Domino after the third time I rearranged his cat room because I needed to keep myself busy.

"Chance?"

I looked up from where I was hunched over my beer to see the girl–I think her name was Caroline, smiling down at me. "Yeah, thanks for meeting me here. Sorry, it's crowded."

There'd been no effort in my appearance tonight. I'd thrown on a hat, a black shirt I wasn't entirely sure was clean, and a pair of work jeans with grass stains all over them. They would forever smell like gasoline after Tyler accidentally dumped it on me while trying to fill the commercial mower we'd had when we started our business.

I didn't stand but motioned to the seat across from me at the small table. "Caroline, right? What are you drinking?"

She took a seat, looking around like she wasn't expecting us to stay. "It's Marilyn, actually. Um, I'll take a Sex on the Beach."

I snorted but disguised it behind a cough as I stood from the table and grabbed my half-empty beer. "Be right back."

While I waited for Big Al, the large bartender who wore a Hawaiian shirt and a look that said *don't fuck with me,* I contemplated if this is how I would always feel about women from now on. Constantly comparing them to Rylee. Finding all their faults and knowing they'd never measure up.

I wondered if this was how Rylee felt after Devon had broken her heart.

When Big Al finally made his way over to me, his intimidating glare turned into a big grin. "Chance! Good to see ya tonight. Whatcha drinking?"

"Yeah, good to see you, too. I'll take another Blue Moon and a Sex on the Beach, please." I leaned on the bar, folding my forearms and resting my weight while I waited.

"Sex on the Beach? Since when does Rylee drink that shit?" He gave me a funny look as he grabbed a glass to pour my beer.

My expression tightened, and the hole in my chest grew as I shook my head. "She doesn't. I'm not here with her."

He paused and gave me a funny look before making the sugary cocktail Marilyn had ordered. "Huh. I thought...ah, never mind. You singing tonight?"

I shook my head. "No. I'm not staying long. I probably shouldn't have even come tonight."

He set the drink before me and took the cash I held out for him. "We got a live one kicking off the evening. Stick around for that, at least." He winked at me as he moved on to the next person after he gave me my change. I left it on the bar and turned back to the table where Marilyn was sitting with her nose scrunched up like she smelt something terrible.

What was it about girls my age not being able to appreciate a good dive bar?

The crowd was thick as I made my way back to the table while the MC welcomed everyone. I had grabbed a small table that was nestled on a platform raised above the rest of the crowd and had an unobstructed view of the stage.

Marilyn flipped her hair with a fake smile as I set her drink in front of her. "Thanks. Do you come here often?"

Her overly big hair was in my way, and I shifted so I could focus on the show as I nodded at her. Every time I moved so I could see, she'd duck her head to try and catch my eye again. "Is everything okay? You don't really seem like you want to be here."

"I don't. I'm sorry, I shouldn't have asked you to come, let alone taken your number at the store. The truth is I was just broken up with and I'm not in a place to date."

I was vaguely aware of the MC introducing

whoever the live performance was as Marilyn smiled and cocked her head. "Sounds like you need a rebound." She reached across the table and ran a finger down my hand as the crowd started to clap.

My hand jerked back on its own, my body physically recoiling at her unwelcome touch. "I'm not interested in using you for a rebound."

Whatever her response was fell on deaf ears as a familiar voice filled the bar. "Thank you, everyone. This is my first time up here. It's a lot more nerve-racking than I thought it would be. Whew. My palms are sweaty."

"Mom's spaghetti!" Someone yelled from the crowd causing laughter to erupt around the room and the familiar voice to chuckle nervously.

My heart seized as I stood, my attention snapping to where Rylee was standing on the stage with some woman I didn't recognize sitting behind her with a guitar. "The original version of this song was sung on this stage a few months ago by someone very special to me. That same someone is here tonight, so I'd like to try a different rendition for him."

I took a few steps to the railing that surrounded the tables. I watched as she paused for a moment before her eyes slowly turned to me. Her pink-painted lips turned up in a smile as she nodded my way. A few people turned to look at me, but I only had eyes for her.

The woman behind her started plucking a few chords, and as the acoustic chords of "Take A

Chance On Me" filled the room, I realized that Rylee was about to sing. As the first few words found my ears, my body went into flight-or-fight mode. My heart wanted to stay while my mind wanted to flee.

She wasn't terrible as she sang, and when she got to the part about the birds, she sent me a smirk at our private joke. And it was too much. Before I realized what I was doing, my feet were moving through the crowd, and I heard her stop singing to call out my name, but I kept moving.

The crowd parted and let me through, murmurs following me as I registered the MC coming back on stage and apologizing for the interruption. I shoved open the door and headed in the direction of my truck. I didn't feel bad about leaving Marilyn behind, and as I heard the door open swiftly behind me, I half expected it to be her, still attempting to get me to take her to my bed.

"Chance! Wait!" Rylee's voice rang out.

My feet stopped before my brain could catch up, and I turned around to see her walking as quickly as her bright pink heels would allow her on the gravel of the parking lot. "You didn't have to run away," she panted as she wiped her palms against her light blue shorts.

She acted like she hadn't broken my heart a few days earlier, and I scoffed, "I had to get you off the stage somehow. I told you that you shouldn't sing karaoke."

Rylee let out a short laugh as she stepped closer.

Tension rippled between us as she said, "It was supposed to be a grand gesture. But I guess I fucked that up, too."

Truthfully, she sounded better on stage than she had in my kitchen. But I wasn't about to tell her that. Why was she here making grand gestures? She'd put me through enough. I couldn't...and wouldn't keep doing the back and forth with her.

"What are you doing here, Rylee?" I asked as I took my hat off and ran my hand through my hair before putting it on backward.

"What's it look like I'm doing, Chance? This is my way of saying I'm sorry. I'm so sorry for everything."

My heart jumped to my throat, and I swallowed thickly. I didn't know if I could do this again with her. I didn't think I'd survive if she took it back one more time. And I didn't want to spend the rest of my life miserable, believing that love could no longer exist after her.

I shook my head as I looked at her. "Rylee, I don't know if I can do this again."

"I know. I know, Chance, and I completely understand if you don't want to. I deserve that, and you deserve the world. And I'm so sorry for thinking that we couldn't be together in order for you to have the life you deserve. It was never my choice to make, and I shouldn't have taken it from you."

It was everything I wish she'd said Tuesday night, and my brain was screaming at me to tell her she was right and that I was done. But the walls I'd built around the hole in my chest started to crumble the longer I stared at her. She looked so hopeful, so beautiful.

So *mine*.

And I knew my mind had been made up the second I saw her on that stage.

Rylee

"Do you think we can just...I don't know, start over?"

My nerves were shot as I watched the emotions play out on his face. I had a hunch he was at war with himself internally, and I couldn't blame him. If he told me no and walked away, I would deserve it.

But he looked contemplative before he stuck his hand out. I looked at it, confused, then realization dawned on me. Relief flooded through my body, and I grabbed it, smiling up at him as we shook hands, not letting go right away, just like the first time we had met.

"I'm Chance. I like cats more than dogs. I own a landscaping business. I have a shitty relationship with my dad, but we're working on it. And I'm in love with a woman who used to date him. But we fucked things up real bad, and I'm not sure we can work it out."

"Well, Chance. I'm Rylee. I can't sing, as you heard back there. I own a bakery slash bar here in town. I went skydiving once, and the only way my boyfriend could get me to jump was to get me off as we did it. He was always pushing me out of my comfort zone, but I think that's one of the things I love most about him. He's a lot younger than me, and I used to date his dad, but here we are."

"Sounds like we're both emotionally taken, then. But if you'd like to come over and have a drink with me at my place...." he trailed off. Our hands were still intertwined, suspended between us, and his thumb started to stroke my knuckle.

"Going to your place on a first date? We just met." I smiled mischievously up at him as I took a step closer.

Chance also came a step closer as he dipped his head a little and said softly, "We did a lot more than have a drink on our first date if I recall."

I swallowed thickly as I took one more step into him, our hands cradled between our chests, mine on his and his on mine so that both of us felt the other's heart pounding. "I missed you."

He sighed in defeat. "I've spent every day wondering if I would spend the rest of my life asking myself, '*what if?*' What if Devon hadn't shown up at my house that day? If we hadn't gone to Sandridge. If I hadn't let my jealousy get the best of me. You'll never know how sorry I am about Abigail."

I laid a finger against his lips to hush him. "Chance, it's okay. It's all in the past now. I want to let go of the past and focus on our future." Then, with complete confidence, I spoke the three words I hadn't said to another man since Devon. "I love you."

His lips broke out in a massive smile behind my finger. I moved my hand to cup his cheek and pulled his head closer to mine. "So, what do you say? Will you take a chance on me? On us?"

Chance wrapped his free hand around my waist, and it felt so good to be in his arms again. So natural. So *right*.

"Baby, I've been taking a chance on us since the day I walked into Sugar and Scotch. I never stopped. I love you, too."

He leaned down and kissed me, and it felt like coming home. His lips moved softly against mine, our hands clenched tighter between us, and we didn't stop until we heard a cough and a nasally, "Oh, dear."

We parted abruptly and looked over to see Bill standing there, holding hands with a pretty blonde who also wore glasses and had her hair pulled up in a scrunchie.

"Well, this is quite awkward. Birdie, this is the one I told you about. This is my ex-girlfriend—Rylee. Rylee, this is my *fiancée,* Birdie," Bill stated.

Chance looked the other way as he laughed into my hair. "Birdie?" he whispered.

I made a shushing noise and giggled as I hit him lightly in the chest. "Hi there, nice to meet you, Birdie."

"Yes, well. I would say the same, but I won't

since you broke poor Bill's heart. Although, your loss is my gain. We're about to leave for the Galapagos islands to go bird-watching. It's truly a dream come true." Her voice was almost as nasally as Bill's, and I had to bite the inside of my cheek to stop myself from laughing.

Chance wasn't even trying to hide it anymore.

Bill bristled and huffed. "Come, Birdie. Let's not let this ruin our evening."

As they walked away, Chance called out, "Good to see you, Bill. Have fun with your birds."

Bill and Birdie both looked affronted as they walked into Pascal's, and Chance and I nearly doubled over in laughter. "Oh my god, did that really just happen?" I asked him, wiping the tears from my eyes.

"We've come full circle. See? It was meant to be." He grinned down at me.

I smiled and wrapped my arms around him again. "We're going to be okay."

He leaned down and kissed me lightly as he returned my embrace, and pulled me closer before he agreed. "Yeah. We are. Come on, let's go home."

EPILOGUE

WHILE WE DID END UP AT CHANCE'S THAT
night–cuddled up with Domino and spending the
following morning having breakfast on the patio with
Gary–we waited another four weeks before packing
up my stuff to move into his house like we'd origi-
nally planned.

Sadie and Tyler were helping us move today, and
as I unpacked a box of trinkets to display in the living
room, I grinned as Sadie and Chance playfully
argued about Gary.

"Have you never seen the movie *Lake Placid*?!"
she shouted at him.

Chance and Tyler looked at each other before
they both shrugged and shook their heads.

"Oh, don't you act all big and bad, Tyler. You
won't go near the thing either, so don't pretend like
you're not bothered by it," Sadie admonished as she

opened a box of shoes and set them aside for the bedroom.

"Can we stop talking about my water puppy like he's a monster?" Chance asked. "And keep it down, would you? He's got good hearing. You're going to hurt his feelings."

"*Our* water puppy," I corrected him.

He grinned at me as Domino meowed from where he was perched on the back of the couch, lazily flicking his tail back and forth as he monitored our progress.

"At least I don't have to worry about you trying to eat me," Tyler said in a baby voice as he moved to pet him. Domino's ears flattened, and he opened his mouth in a silent hiss as Tyler followed up with, "Why don't you like me?"

"You're talking shit about his best buddy. They know when you're not being nice to other animals," I told him. But my words were ignored as he honed in on Sadie, who was checking her phone with a frown.

"Everything okay?" he asked her, all the playfulness gone from his voice.

Chance wrapped his arms around me from behind and nuzzled my neck before he whispered in my ear, "I'm ready to start our first night with you all moved in. Make them go away."

But Sadie was already moving to grab her things. "I need to jet up to the city for a few days. I gotta go if I'm gonna make the next flight. Let me know how dinner with daddy Devon goes tomorrow." She came over, hugged me, and kissed my cheek before hugging Chance and then moving toward the door.

"Hey, what about me?" Tyler asked, his tone a little lighter than it had been earlier.

She turned with her hand on the doorknob and grinned at him. "Bye, pup."

"She wants me," he exclaimed after she shut the door.

"Okay, Tyler. You can entertain those delusions at your own home. Time to go." Chance grabbed him by the back of his hoodie and pulled him toward the door.

"I thought we were ordering pizza! And watching movies! Rylee, what is *Lake Placid* about?" he shouted behind him.

I laughed as Chance grabbed his keys from where they hung on the wall and tossed them to Tyler. "I have something else in mind for dinner tonight," he said as he turned and fixed me with his heated gaze.

My lower belly instantly flooded with warmth, and I bit my lip as I dropped a photo of Chance and me singing karaoke back into the box I was unpacking.

It turns out that when you love someone, you really will put up with all their faults, even if they aren't the greatest at singing.

"Aww, man. I didn't need to hear that!" Tyler whined as he pulled his hood up while Chance shoved him out the door. "Have fun, you two!"

Once the door was closed again, Chance turned to me, and his voice dropped as he said, "Oh, I intend to."

I walked over to him, and he wrapped his arms around me again, leaning down to lay a chaste kiss on my lips. "Are you happy?" he asked.

My arms wound around his neck, and I pulled him closer as I replied. "The happiest I've ever been."

"Good," he said softly before he kissed me again, deeper this time. His hands moved down to my thighs as he effortlessly picked me up and started to walk to our bedroom.

Once we got there, he gently laid me on the bed and broke our kiss to whisper, "I'm going to spend the rest of my life making sure you're the happiest woman in the world."

"As long as I have you, that's all I need. And you? Are you happy?" I asked him, staring into those pools of scotch that I adored so much.

Chance grinned down at me and nuzzled my nose. "I've never been happier, baby."

And as if we'd asked them as well, Domino chimed in with a meow as Gary let out his own loud rumble from his place on the patio.

READY FOR MORE?

Keep reading for a sneak peek at book two of the Sugar and Scotch Duet, Sweet as Sin.

PROLOGUE

SADIE

Most women in my position would kill for the life I have.

A forty-seven-year-old former model turned millionaire's wife. I get to do what I want when I want. Invest as much money in any pet projects I might have, take as many vacations as I please, and don't even have to have dinner on the table when my husband gets home from work.

Sounds great, doesn't it?

But after almost twenty years, it takes a toll on you. You age out of the career because there is always someone younger, prettier, or cheaper to take your place. You realize your friends aren't really friends at all, just people who want to attach themselves like leeches to your good name and interminable amounts of money. You're lucky to come out on the other side of the industry with one good friend, let alone a group. The vacations turn sullen and solitary because you get tired of paying for everything for the so-called friends, and your husband is always too busy working.

The loving husband who once looked at you with nothing but adoration and pure unadulterated lust in his eyes. The man who told you it would always be you who held his heart in the palm of your hand. The same hand that sported a vintage emerald cut blue diamond set in platinum. It signified the old money from which said husband hailed–and old money meant old ideals.

The plentiful vacations and romantic dinners turned into work trips that '*I wouldn't enjoy*' or were '*men-only, no wives allowed.*' But the next morning's gossip rag showed proof that while the wives weren't allowed, escorts apparently were.

"You'll get used to it, dear. Let the men play with their toys. After all, no one said we couldn't have our fun too." His mother once said to me before her untimely death.

Once you get over the initial embarrassment and learn to act like you already knew your husband stayed the night in some swanky hotel with a woman–or two–half your age, you *do* get used to it. And you find ways to cope.

My coping mechanism happened to be food and sun. So, I bought myself a condo right on the beach in sunny Jacksonville, Florida. The bright cream walls and soft blue accents were my home away from home in the concrete jungle that was New York

City. The first night in Jacksonville, I took myself to dinner at a cute little waterfront restaurant that had a patio that was lit up with torches and framed with low bushes of the best-smelling azaleas.

When you're a model, they don't let you eat cake. Or at least they didn't when I was one. Cake is my coping method. Especially cupcakes, because they are compact and cute. You can make them into little sandwiches and stuff them entirely in your mouth on a particularly bad day when your phone is blowing up with the latest gossip about what–or who– your husband has been doing while you're out of town.

When I tell you this restaurant had the best damn cake I've ever had in my life, I mean every single word of praise for the mini delightful confections. They had these things from a pop-up bakery called Caketails. Little shot glasses that were full of cake and cream and fruit that came in multiple different flavors that just exploded in your mouth.

Caketails were worth investing money in—something to keep me busy and away from New York, I decided. So, of course, I hunted down the woman who made them and forced her to become my friend and give me all her secret recipes.

She didn't give me her recipes, but she did become the first genuine friend I'd had in a long, long time. Together, we achieved her dream of opening a bakery/cafè that turned into a small plates/bar in the evening.

Sugar and Scotch, we called it.

That was three years ago, and the place quickly became a huge success. I take care of the business portion of it–thanks to taking online classes and receiving a business degree the moment I realized my modeling career was coming to an end in my mid-thirties. And she, Rylee, takes care of all the rest.

We make a good team. It was us against the world; the sky was the limit. But then she started dating her much younger boyfriend, Chance. And with Chance came his best friend, Tyler, who was also in his mid-twenties.

With Tyler came the memory of my mother-in-law's words to me years before. *No one said we couldn't have our fun too.*

But Tyler was the dangerous kind of fun. The kind that looks at you like you hold up the sun and the moon, and he wants to drop to his knees and worship between your legs because he thinks you're a goddess. The kind that drinks down every last drop and then fills you up again so he can start over. That ruins you for any other man. That brands himself on your soul.

Tyler was the kind of fun you didn't want to give up. So I didn't want to indulge...even a little.

But fuck if the persistent bastard wasn't like a custard-filled golden cupcake that I wanted to stuff in my mouth every single time I saw him.

CHAPTER ONE

SADIE

"Does it feel tight?"

"Yeah."

"Okay, squeeze it a little, and then go slow."

"It feels better if I go faster."

"Slow down! It's messy when you go fast."

"So bossy. That's fine. More for me to lick up later."

"You like it when I'm bossy. Your movements are awkward. Doesn't that feel funny?"

"No. It feels just fine to me. I may not be as good at this as you are, but my results are undeniably delicious."

"And undeniably ugly," Rylee said, swiping a finger through the bright pink frosting on the cupcake I was piping.

"Hey! I worked hard on that!" I cried and batted Rylee's hand away.

"Hard at making a mess so you can eat all the unsellable treats," Rylee laughed as she broke a chunk of the cupcake off and popped it into her mouth.

I grabbed one as well, the chocolate cake giving easily as I tore it in half, squeezed some raspberry buttercream on it, and mashed the halves together before stuffing it in my mouth.

Rylee raised an eyebrow at my squirrel cheeks and swallowed her bite. "Do you wanna talk about it?"

"Talk about what?" I muttered around the cupcake, my words barely discernible.

Rylee's eyes flitted to the iPad on the table, where the bright screen glowed with a photo of my husband leaving a restaurant with his hand on the lower back of some petite, pretty brunette.

The headline on the article read, '*Scott Tailor steps out with another woman?*' With a byline of, '*Wife of multi-millionaire hasn't been seen in the city in weeks. Trouble in paradise?*'

Wife of....

They hadn't even bothered to use my name until the actual article. I'd been reduced to '*the scorned wife of*' and '*former model and trophy wife of.*' More and more gossip columns had been popping up lately —a new one for every summons from my *dear* husband that I ignored.

"I don't understand why you put up with it,

Sade. Why don't you just leave him?" Rylee asked as she reached over and shut the keyboard case that the iPad rested in.

The noise from the bakery bar we owned filtered through the double doors leading from the bar to the kitchen where we currently were. It was lunchtime, and the afternoon rush that came in to grab sandwiches and soups and sweet treats to give them a sugar boost to get through the rest of their workdays was in full swing.

It was a sound that made me happy. To know that Rylee and I had created a space that people enjoyed occupying during their break from their humdrum jobs. To know that we supplied them with freedom, if only for a little while, and put smiles on their faces.

None of it would have been possible without the money I'd invested in it.

So, I gave my best friend a tight smile and answered, "You know I like the comfort of my life, Ry. If I tried to leave him, he'd make my life miserable. He'd take the condo, and you know he'd try to take this place."

"We're doing just fine. We can take out a loan to pay back the money of his that you invested into it. And aren't you entitled to alimony? It's not like he could try and fight you if you filed and said it was because he's cheating. It's splashed all over the New York gossip columns every week!"

I snorted. "He's Scott Tailor. He'd probably be able to convince a judge it was *me* who was cheating on *him,* so what other choice did he possibly have but to find comfort in the bosom of all the pretty young things he parades around the city?"

A pair of midnight eyes flashed in my mind for a moment. The gentle touch of soft lips against mine. Cedar, sweet mint, and a rich, breathy tenor whispering, *"It can be our little secret."*

"So fucking stupid. I hate this for you," Rylee murmured as she started piping cupcakes the way they were meant to be piped.

I didn't respond, lost in my thoughts. I don't know how much time passed, with me staring at nothing and her working on bakery items before she gently cleared her throat.

"Anything new on the Tyler front?"

Tyler Michaelson. Best friend of her boyfriend, Chance. Both of them skirted twenty years our junior and were—*are*—relentless in their pursuit. Chance and Rylee had been dating for nearly six months, but it had been a long twisted road of Jerry Springer bullshit before their relationship finally settled and secured.

Long story short, Chance was the son of Rylee's former high school boyfriend, who broke her heart when he got Chance's mother pregnant. No, Chance hadn't known who Rylee was—and vice versa—when they met. Yes, Rylee was utterly mortified when she found out. No, neither she, Chance, nor Devon—Chance's dad— took it well.

Yes, love prevailed. And six months later, here we are. He's going to propose soon, and she has no idea. But I know she'll say yes.

During all this, Chance's best friend Tyler had been doing everything in his power to woo me. Yes, I said woo. From the second he walked into the bar to grab Chance away from flirting with Rylee, from the moment we laid eyes on each other, he's been calling me his future wife.

He's tall, tanned, dark-haired, and treats me like a goddess—everything I love in a man. And at first, I was annoyed. I'm married, and Tyler was a temptation being dangled in front of my face like a cat with a mouse on a string.

But he'd become a friend over the last few months. Someone to talk to and confide in. Since Rylee spent the majority of her time with Chance now, I'd found myself quite lonely; and as if he knew that what I really needed was a shoulder to lean on, Tyler had really been there for me.

He was wild and carefree. But for me, he could be profound and insightful. And I sometimes found myself daydreaming about what it would be like to leave my husband and dive headfirst into the world of the twenty-six-year-old.

But I was a creature of comfort. Nearly twenty years in my multiple lavish homes and the ability to do whatever I wanted whenever I wanted didn't have me running toward a life of struggle and working myself to death.

Sure, the bar was popular, and we were doing just fine financially. But I'd have to work seven days a week, open to close, just to afford the dues on my one-point-two million dollar condo on the beach.

Tyler owned half of a landscaping company, with Chance owning the other half. And while they were doing just fine with their business, even combining our incomes wouldn't allow me to live the life I liked.

Yet, sometimes I wanted to think about it. To let those little whispers of secrets and the passing soft touches get under my skin.

But I shouldn't have even been entertaining thoughts of that nature.

Because I wasn't my husband. Why be married if you were just going to cheat all the time? If he had been anyone else, I would have left him, but I'd been content to let him do his thing while I did mine and spent his money. Let him make an ass out of himself.

"Tyler and I are just friends, Ry. You know that." I gathered my things. I didn't want to have this conversation again, and I had errands to run before I had to be back for the bar shift later in the evening.

"One day, he's going to wear you down," she sang, her attention not leaving the cake she was now decorating. I didn't answer, and her soft laughter followed me as I went out the back of the kitchen.

She didn't deserve my attitude, and I was only

irritated because I knew there was truth to her statement.

A fucking dildo only did the job so many times before you wanted the real thing. And after weeks of my husband being photographed with various young women, I sure as fuck wasn't going to run back to New York and sit on his dick.

AFTERWORD

I hope you enjoyed Chance and Rylee's story! Right away, I knew I wanted to set their story in Florida. Sandridge is based super loosely on New Smyrna where I spent a lot of time as a kid during summer break. My grandparents used to own a home there and so that's also what I based the layout of Chance and Tyler's homes on.

Fun fact number one, Gary was based on a real life gator that would come into my grandparents' yard and my grandpa would actually grab it by the tail and bring it back to its swamp.

Fun fact number two, I got the idea for the skydiving date because it happened to me in real life. Sadly, I didn't get the O at the end but I did have a man take me as a surprise and the only reason he told me on the way was because my mom wouldn't get off the phone until he swore he wasn't taking me somewhere to murder me.

It was a lot of fun bringing this to life and I cannot wait for you to read about Sadie and Tyler next.

And did you catch the small subtle hint that tied this story to Where the Flowers Bloom? Let me know if you did!

ACKNOWLEDGMENTS

First and foremost, thank YOU for taking a chance on me and reading my books. Indie authors would be nothing without our readers. So thank you to the entire book community.

HUGE thank you, as always, to A.R. Rose, who is not only my book bestie but is also the only reason I can ever figure anything out when it comes to self-publishing. Can't wait for Taylor Swift in August, friend.

My alpha, and new book bestie, Jessica. You are NEVER getting rid of me, so tell Kegan we're in a committed relationship now. But seriously, I could absolutely not have done this without you. Thank you for being my friend and my writing partner. The person who pulls all-nighters with me and who I tell everything to all day, every day.

My street team, thank you for hyping me up.

And last but not least, thank you to my husband, Joe, for putting up with my mood swings when I fall behind my deadline. And for bringing me snacks when I refuse to leave my writing cave.

ABOUT THE AUTHOR

D.L. Darby lives with her husband, dog, and cat, in Anchorage, Alaska. When she's not at her salon or writing, she's usually outside hiking (when the weather allows it), snuggled up with her animals reading a book, or filming a ridiculous amount of TikTok's for the upcoming month.

You can join her reader group, D.L. Darby's Darlings on Facebook. Or follow her on Instagram and/or TikTok @d.l.darby_author

www.dldarbyauthor.com

Made in United States
Troutdale, OR
11/24/2023

14910304R00170